W9-AYR-624

PIONEER BREED

Books by Glenn R. Vernam

INDIAN HATER

PIONEER BREED

PIONEER BREED

GLENN R. VERNAM

DOUBLEDAY & COMPANY, INC.
GARDEN CITY, NEW YORK
1972

This book is entirely fictitious. Any resemblance to persons living or dead is purely coincidental.

First Edition

Library of Congress Catalog Card Number 77-157632

Printed in the United States of America

TO JUANITA

A salute to courage,
man's highest virtue

PIONEER BREED

CHAPTER 1

Rance Hardig hitched up the single gallus of his frayed canvas overalls, his lanky length sagging against the handle of the homemade hoe. One hand pushed the beads of sweat up against his bristly, straw-colored hair. His sky-blue eyes drifted back down the row of freshly dug potatoes, their pale brown skins looking like varnished globules under the afternoon sun. Twenty bushels or more, he judged, and another full row to go. With the turnips, onions, carrots, and cabbage already piled in the unfinished roothouse, the Hardigs stood to eat to fattening during the coming winter. Rance grinned his slow smile of satisfaction as he straightened up to aim his hoe at another hill.

Early fall in Oregon's upper Rogue River Valley of 1852 was a time for mind and senses to luxuriate in the extravaganza of rainbow-stained foliage; to savor the soft breath of a sun-warmed breeze sighing down from the newly frosted heights of the overhanging Siskiyou Peaks. Willow and cottonwoods flaunted their golden glow against the green of fir and pine, as if trying to outrival the red of sumac and vine maple crowding against the ripening cornfield.

Rance swung his hoe with the detached absorption of one wholly in tune with his surroundings. The drone of insects, the old woodpecker's steady drumming on a hemlock snag, the muted discussions of the mallard family voicing an undertone to the creek's rippling song, all blended into a soothing melody that lent strength to weary muscles intruding on the mind.

The hoe continued its rhythmic advance from one potato hill to another, pausing only while a bare toe shoved an elusive tuber apart from its earthly concealment. Rance's thoughts idly recalled Pa's decision to pass up the Willamette Valley in favor of the Jacksonville gold fields. With the talk of the recent gold discovery painting shining dreams in everyone's mind, this last leg of their journey hadn't seemed like much of a trip, after the previous half-year's haul from Missouri. However, their failure to find the promised wealth in paying quantities had made the move look like a gut-shot effort. That is, it did at first. But Pa was not the kind to knuckle down and take a whipping. Almost before they had time to do any fretting over the way things turned out, he had located this little creek basin back in the hills and filed a donation claim. Now it was beginning to look like Pa had been right all along, even if it had seemed crazy for him to switch suddenly onto the idea that there was more real wealth in growing things than chasing luck underground.

Maybe there was something to his notion that nobody ever saw a mole make any progress in life beyond the size of its last hole. Come to think of it, Pa's logic seldom missed fire. This place was the latest proof of that. This first year alone had seen the lower end of the meadow in crop, and almost as much brush land across the creek cleared for another spring's planting. With more and more hungry people coming to the mines, everything they could raise would net them their share of the gold that was gouged out of the earth. And theirs would be a sure thing; no blind gambling with a tricky hole in the ground. Yes, sir, Pa sure had the right of it, when all was said and done.

Rance grinned happily, tugging at his bristly forelock. He

lifted his hoe for attack on another potato hill. Ma would sure be seeing stars when she found out how the crop was turning out. She had speculated heavy on that new winter dress, if they had a mite extra to sell. Now with half a crop more than they would need for their own eating, she might be able to even get the new boughten shoes and coat that had tickled her fancy that last trip to Jacksonville. Ma would be right good-looking if she didn't have to wear sloppy old Indian moccasins and a coat half made over with canvas patches. He spared another glance back down the row.

"Yes, sir," he reflected, "there would be a right smart plenty to fix her up proper-like, the prices the miners were willing to shell out for anything in the vegetable line."

A great surge of happiness surged up in his throat as one foot automatically rooted out another reluctant potato. Pure joy puckered his lips, starting their search for the opening notes of "Oh! Susanna." He wished he didn't always have such a tussle getting started on that tune.

He backed up for a fresh start just in time to have the squeaky notes driven back down his throat by a woman's shrill scream. The voice was still ringing in his ears when Pa's old Hawken rifle drove a second wave of sound down the valley.

The hoe went rolling as Rance dived headfirst through the double line of creek willows that hid the long slope up to the cabin. The wilderness-bred instinct of an Oregon Territory settler needed no pondering to know that trouble was afoot. Bad trouble! Ma wasn't the screaming kind; and Pa didn't go for needless shooting when he had work to do. A bear, maybe, or—or—but there had been no sign of Indians this far south, for months. His breath whistled in his throat as his callused feet beat a tattoo around fresh stumps and unburned brush piles.

The cabin came into view a long hundred yards up the slope. Its single door swayed in rhyme to the gentle drone of its wooden hinge pins set into lintel and sill. Rance swept his eyes back and forth across the slope as he ran. Everything looked peaceable enough. Smoke spirals climbed lazily from the rough stone chimney to mingle with the soft blue haze of Indian summer. The busy woodpecker was still hammering at the old hemlock snag. Rance thought he caught a suspicious sound from beyond the house, but couldn't be sure, the way his lungs were pumping. Anyway, there was no further noise. He swiped the unruly lock of hair out of his eyes and raced for the open door.

Nor did he stop there. His rush carried him on across the room. One hand automatically reached the double-barreled, caplock shotgun down from the deer-horn rack before he paused for a swift glance around the cabin. A pot of venison, simmering gently over a bed of coals in the newly finished fireplace, only made the empty quietness pinch down tighter. Ma's brush broom lay in the middle of the packed-earth floor, where she had evidently dropped it in a hurry. Rance bent double and ducked across to the unshuttered square hole which served as a back window. Cautiously, he raised his eyes above the sill.

"God help us!" His suddenly whitened lips framed the words as his sickened stomach wrenched convulsively.

That single glance told him the whole gruesome story. His thin face pinched down to a gray mask as he pictured the five Indians bursting out of the salal brush above the springhouse while Pa's back was turned. Ma must have seen them first, her scream bringing the rifle into action only at the last moment. She lay beside the sprawling brush pile, her arms wrapped around a bunch of fire boughs beneath her, as though trying to hide her hideously gashed face. Pa's slumped body was still half straddle of the log he had been hewing. The ugly dark stain surrounding the twin arrow shafts protruding from his back matched well the reddened chopping-axe lying across one of the two gory figures in front of him. The split skulls of both Indians gaped in sickening tribute to a desperate adversary. The rifle, fallen against the log a few feet to the right, would account for the farther Indian sprawled head down in a laurel bush.

Rance sucked in his breath. Hard! Red-hot irons seemed to be pushing on the backs of his eyeballs as he centered them on the two remaining Indians. Rogues, he guessed. Pa had heard that some of their young bucks had been waving tomahawks up on the North Fork during the last full moon. Nothing much had come of it, however. Pa had put it down as just a flash in the pan, not worth getting het up about, especially this far south. This bunch was probably something of the same kind, a few glory hunters on the prowl for any easy prey. Easy prey! Rance swallowed the bile in his throat as he eared back the big shotgun hammers and shoved the gun up over the windowsill.

The two uninjured Rogues, who had apparently avoided hand-to-hand conflict, paused beside the hewed log. The larger one bent over briefly, coming up with a red-crowned braid of long yellow hair in his hand. His companion reached sidewise for the settler's rifle, a wolfish grin lighting his face. Here was a prize indeed. But not for him! The full charge of buckshot caught him under the chin to stop his gloating exclamation. The contents of the other barrel struck the larger man just above his greasy G-string as he straightened to shake the yellow braid defiantly at the cabin.

Rance watched the suddenly stilled bodies for an instant before reaching for the shot pouch and powder horn. Pa was always mighty firm about reloading before walking up on downed critters. Besides, there might be other lurkers back in the brush. A body couldn't be too careful. He tamped down the loads and fitted new percussion caps on the nipples.

The danger, however, seemed to be over. A half hour of watching and listening brought no hint of further trouble. A quick scout around the cabin and through the salal clump persuaded him that he had guessed right about the five raiders being a lone group. With the gun still under his arm, he rummaged in the shed for a shovel.

Thanks to a mind frozen in the merciful blank numbness of shock, he was able to go about the needful task doggedly and unthinkingly. The grave had to be wide enough for two, blind instinct told him. Luckily, the ground was fairly soft where it leveled off east of the spring. Weary muscles responded gratefully to Ma's light weight. It had been quite a tussle to move Pa over to the grave and lay him out respectable-like. It was a sight of comfort to find the arrow wounds in his back didn't show. And Ma looked almost like herself, right peaceful, in fact, after he had wiped her face clean and plastered the scalp back in place, with the yellow braid down over her breast. The hardest part was shoveling the dirt back over them. He guessed he might not have been able to handle that part if it hadn't been for the chunk of wagon canvas he had found to tuck over and around them. They looked almost like the last time he had seen them, snugged down in bed for the night, just before he blew out the candle and followed a strip of moonlight across to his own leanto bedroom. Mayhaps he wasn't seeing the thing in a rightful manner. It was hard to tell what was proper thinking, when a body's mind had gone off somewhere and hid. Still, everything had kind of righted itself after he had rounded up the grave mound and read, with slow, halting lips, a few verses from Pa's Bible book. Pa always held that some Bible reading would smooth out most troubles. And it seemed like Pa was right this time, near as he could tell, drained out like he was till each thought felt like something being hauled up out of a well.

CHAPTER 2

It was a long, orange-tinted finger of morning sunshine, probing the square window hole, that brought a first response from the bowed shoulders hunched over the split-log table set on four legs of sapling pine. It trailed a sympathetic touch across the faded homespun shirt, as though reluctant to rouse the silent figure. For a moment, it dallied hesitantly, its golden glow outlining the tousled mop of straw-colored hair resting on crossed forearms. Rance stirred sluggishly, like some hibernating creature scenting the first warm breath of spring. The soft caress of sunlight lingered tenderly on one dirt-smeared cheek gouged deep by ragged white tear furrows. He stirred again, as if in reply, nuzzling his face into the shirtsleeve.

"Aw right, Ma," he muttered thickly. "'M gittin' up. I—I—"

He lifted his head groggily, grimy knuckles rubbing at his eyes. For a moment, his undirected ears probed the eerie quietness, then returning consciousness slapped him suddenly across the face with cold realization. The brutal shock of memory widened his eyes, half lifting him out of the rawhide-bottomed chair. Misery gripped his throat with clammy fingers as his gaze moved slowly around the room.

No, there was no mistake! Yesterday's horror rose in all its hideous reality to banish any suggestion of nightmarish dreams. The awful truth stared at him from the pot of venison hanging above the pile of dead ashes in the fireplace, its skim of cold grease still undisturbed. As if in confirmation, the brush broom mutely signaled its abandonment from the middle of the floor. A partly knit sock snuggled orphanlike against the sheltering ball of yarn in the low cherrywood rocker brought from Missouri. Pa's long rifle and the caplock shotgun leaned companionably against the wall, where he had stood them the night before. Rance swallowed hard against the long shudder that tore at his insides. One hand scrubbed hard at his tear-filled eyes.

"Oh, God!" he croaked. "Ma an' Pa, both! And they never had a chance!"

He dropped his head back on his arms while dry, wracking sobs shook his slim body.

One hour, two, while a yellowish-brown spider patiently eyed the gyrations of three lazily droning flies. The woodpecker started his drumming again, as the jerky breathing slowly eased itself beneath the hunched shoulders. The warm autumn sun shifted its benevolent rays to the narrow strip of tanned skin between untrimmed hair and frayed shirt collar. A plaintive bellow voiced its distress from the log barn beyond the cabin. Rance pulled himself slowly upright, rubbing bloodshot eyes with the back of his hand, as another bawl of grievance echoed from the barn.

"I reckon's how I'd best be tendin' to things," he told himself uncertainly. "Pa would be right smart put out was I to let the chores slide, just 'cause he's gone."

He shoved the rawhide-bottomed chair back and stood up. His eyes made another slow circuit of the room before he bent to pick up the brush broom. Walking with the stiffened gait of an old man, he shuffled across the floor to stand the broom in its rightful place behind the door. For another moment he stood, eyes staring at nothing, while he scratched absently at the smear of dried clay on the back of his hand. Then, still moving woodenly, he crossed to the fireplace and knelt to uncover the few live coals beneath the cold ashes. Pure habit led his fingers to the handful of shavings in the split kindling basket. Carefully spreading them over the coals, he gently blew the embers into life, all the while feeling as though something outside himself was directing each move.

But with the thin curl of resinous smoke rising softly against his nostrils, youth and nature reasserted themselves. The warm fragrance of burning pine slivers revived the aroma of boiled venison to remind Rance of the hours since yesterday's dinner. His stomach stirred in ready confirmation of the long neglect. Abused muscles, too, would not be denied a note of complaint for the wearisome job of grave digging, alone and unaided. The actual burials had been no less punishing. Even dragging the enemy casualties into a handy stump hole and shoveling dirt over them had been a backbreaking task, lasting long after dark. A weary sigh rode his breath into the open as he laid a crisscross of heavier wood over the thin blaze and swung the stew kettle into position. He filled the coffeepot and hung it on the back of the crane.

"Should be boiled up agin I finish milkin' old Brockle," he reasoned. "Pa was allus one to hold on a man's first duty bein' toward dependent livestock. Poor old cow! I'll bet her bag's nigh to bust from me forgettin' her last night."

He walked out into the sunlight, only to stand motionless with one hand resting absently on the rim of the upturned milk pail. Hot, bitter pain welled up in his eyes as his glance drifted across the fresh mound of earth crowning the little flat below the spring. Both fists knotted themselves into bony white knobs, while strangled sobs twisted his face into a tortured caricature. He suddenly grabbed the bucket under one arm and stumbled, almost running, toward the barn.

He didn't know how he would have made out, thinking on it later, if old Brockle hadn't furnished something more vital to claim his attention. Ma had evidently shut the cow in the corral when she came up to the barn before the Indian attack. Left overnight without milking, and no doubt disgusted with being held captive long after the heifer calf, the gray mare, and the Buck mule had wandered off to the pasture, she had tried to climb over the split-rail fence. Now she was hung up halfway over the fence, one hind leg trapped between two of the lower rails.

Rance upended the bucket over a post and went to look for a rope, his sorrow shoved into the background by immediate needs. This was serious! The cow might break a leg any minute. He loped back around the barn, rope in hand. His mind only had room for the best way of rescuing the animal, without further damage.

It proved to be quite a job, at that. With her head tied to a post, to prevent any floundering, it was all he could do to slowly work the rails out from under her weight, chanting soothing assurances all the while. When she decided to lie down on the last rail, which had been supporting her body, he was forced to get the axe and chop it in two midway of its span. It was a sorely disgruntled cow that switched her tail defiantly as he led her into the barn to run a hand over the swollen udder.

Yet there was no serious damage done. He was thankful for that. He couldn't afford to have a crippled cow on his hands. It was bad enough to have to rebuild the corral fence.

It seemed as though fate had deliberately schemed to keep him busy that day. Mayhaps it was like Pa often spoke about busy hands easing a troubled mind. At any rate, he found himself hard put to do all the needful things before night caught him out on a limb. Just redding up the chores waiting for him at the springhouse, that Pa had rocked up around the end of the gouged-out log trough set to catch the water coming from the spring, ran into half a forenoon's work. There was the new milk to strain into the setting pans. This led to the discovery that yesterday's milk was ripe for skimming, while the week's cream stood ready for the dasher churn. Any gawk could see it wouldn't nowise do to let the butter-making go, what with the fine price butter would bring over at the Jacksonville mines.

"And there's the spuds still layin' out there waitin' to be sunburnt," he reminded himself. "Not takin' inta account the nigh onto a full row not dug yet."

This brought up a vision of the roothouse yet to be finished before the vegetables could be stored. Rance gulped the rest of his belated breakfast and poured water over his dirty dishes in the hewed-out log dish trough. He squinted at the sun. Half the forenoon already gone. Mayhaps he'd best just bunch the spuds up and cover them with the wilted vines; the roothouse wouldn't be much help till he got a roof on it. Anyhow, fixing that fence was the first thing. And it had better be done before old Brockle came up for the night's milking, unless he craved more trouble.

The following days were no less demanding. Rance found little time for grief. The scanty moments he had for thought were invariably captured by the multitude of tasks crying for attention. Nights were the worst, when stark despair crowded in on him to flaunt its hopeless futility. The only saving grace was his numb weariness, which usually left him with ambition to do no more than cook up a meal of sorts before surrendering to drugged sleep. Each morning seemed bent on whittling the day down to half the time he needed if he was to get anywhere.

"Might be the smart thing was I to pull out an' find a job

over at the mines," he speculated idly, taking a breather while midway of shoveling a frost-proof cover of dirt over the poles and brush that roofed the roothouse. "I could work reg'lar hours an' buy my board. Still, I doubt if Pa would hold with that, now't we've got such a good start here. Anyhow, what'd become of old Brockle an' her heifer calf, the gray mare an' the Buck mule? There ain't much sale for critters, an' they couldn't be left to a starvin' winter."

He shook his head and put the idea away for all time. Pa held that a body could make out somehow, if he humped his back to it. Besides, a home was not a thing to run out on. The only way to do was stiffen up and try to be the kind of a hand Pa always hoped for.

He went back to his shoveling. His mind had already turned to the problem of making a door for the dirt-roofed dugout built into the hillside. It would be easy to log both sides of the front up tight enough to shut out the frost; but a trifling, scrannelly door could let in enough cold to make all his other work useless. If he just had some good boughten boards, now, enough to box up a double door with space for stuffing the inside full of something! But wishing was a sorry horse, fitting for only a weak mind to ride, as Pa always claimed. No, he guessed he'd best drop that kind of thinking down a rathole, while he laid out something that stood to really serve his purpose. Now if he was to get some poles, say, and face them to make a frame? And it wouldn't be hard to rive out a smattering of shakes to cover the frame on both sides. That would leave plenty of room for all the grass stuffing needful for shutting out the cold. He nodded in satisfaction over his reasoning and returned to the shoveling. A body could do a sight of things, once he really yoked his mind to it.

Making the roothouse door gave him the idea of building a roof over the stack of hay he and Pa had so laboriously scythed down in the meadow and hauled up to the barn. It was claimed that this country got a lot of snow and rain during the winter. Now that it had settled down, the little rick of hay looked like a mighty piddling amount to last four critters till spring. To have some of it go bad from wetting could easy mean short rations for the stock. A pole frame hitched onto the barn and covered with shakes, same as he had made the door, should stave off any damage to the feed supply. Also, it would make a nice place to pile the corn fodder, soon as he got it cut. He had been kind of worrying about weather damage to the fodder, left standing out in the shock. Pa had apparently let that idea get past him. It gave a swelling of pride to think about coming up with something a man liken Pa had overlooked.

Of course, it would have been a sight better and easier if he had some nails to peg the shakes onto the poles, but a body couldn't have everything the first year on a new donation claim. Anyhow, the long, slim poles, lashed down with willow withes over each course of shakes, made a pretty substantial job. Right down tidy, too, he congratulated himself, surveying the new structure a week later. Besides protecting his feed, it made the barn look more like something that had come to stay. He pulled at his straw-colored forelock. The whole thing had turned out to be just another roothouse door on a bigger scale. It was uncommon queer how an idea could branch out that way, like a sapling shoot.

Meanwhile, there was a scad of wood to be cut and stacked up against the coming winter. Rance was sure glad Pa'd had the foresight to skid that bunch of logs up to the cabin, while they were clearing the bottom. That made it right handy for chopping into fireplace lengths at odd moments, instead of having to lay out straight time on rustling it out of the brush. This was quite a comfort, the way everything else was bent on overcrowding him.

CHAPTER 3

Rance found that nearly everything locked horns with something else. The new shed demanded that the corn be cut and stacked inside before the fall rains set in. Then the potato, onion, carrot, and turnip crops yielded a surplus that was three times what he could use. Likewise, the butter keg, set in the springhouse, was full to overrunning. It all wrapped itself up into cause for a trip to town, where he could exchange his products for store-boughten things needful to see him through the winter.

He squinted at the gray streak in the east as he hitched the gray mare and the Buck mule to the wagon. One hand fingered his jaw thoughtfully, where Pa's razor had left only two little nicks. He was glad he had the forethought to clean himself up and load the wagon the night before. A daylight start was a most needful thing, if he aimed to get into Jacksonville in time to do his trading before night. This last was also something of a must, necessary to his starting the home trip by first light the following morning. A body dassent do any tarrying, slow as the going was over a road that stood as only a wheel mark. Anyhow, two regular milkings for old Brockle to be calf-sucked would be hurtful nough. He heaved himself up over the front wheel with a sigh. It seemed like everything he did only put the gad to him to get on with something else.

"Be almost glad when winter shuts down," he muttered. "It might give me a chance to ketch up on a few things."

The ride to town, however, proved lazily restful. "Nigh pleasurable as a real layoff," he told himself, relaxing under the warmth of the late autumn sun climbing up over the eastern mountains.

He munched on a belated breakfast of venison steaks and cold biscuits as he swayed to the jolting of the wagon. The wheel tracks from their spring migration up the valley and the midsummer trip out to Jacksonville for supplies wound through the timber and forded the creek a couple of times. He guessed Pa had been right crafty to lay out as good a trail as he did, being first to put a wheel through this new country. The occasional rocks and chuckholes did kind of give a body's liver more or less of a workout, but he guessed there was no law said a man had to keep himself plastered to the plank-board seat every minute. Anyhow, such things were just little oddments you couldn't rightly fret about, considering the chore of making out in a plumb new country. He tugged at his forelock and whistled a few bars of "Oh, Susanna" as his gaze drifted idly over the kaleidoscope of fall colors flung like some fabled Persian shawl across the hillside.

He made good time, despite the rough going. Still, it was nice to finally get down on the fairly level floor of the main valley. He leaned back with the feeling of a job well accomplished, when he dropped into the twin ruts that snaked their way through the shoulder-high grass. By the time they turned into the broader roadway that the more progressive citizens were beginning to call Oregon Street, the sun had finished lowering itself behind the timbered ridges of the Coast Range.

"The town's really been buildin' up this summer," he observed, casting a glance at the new stonework building going up next to the log cabin that carried the sign of Peter Britt, Photograph Studio. "Shore wish Pa'd been favored in gettin' that picture of him an' Ma that he talked about. It woulda been a faultless thing to treasure, had they not been cut off afore the chance to pleasure themselves thataway."

He swallowed the lump in his throat, turning his back on the studio to study the many new log and rough-board buildings checkerboarding the flat. There were even a couple of two-story structures, looking to be of shiny red brick, on up the street. Yes, sir, Jacksonville was getting to be a real sure 'nough city these days!

He swung his team in to the hitching rack under the sign of J. R. BRUNNER & BRO., GENERAL MERCHANDISE. PRODUCE AND HIDES TAKEN IN EXCHANGE. This was the store Pa held to be the fairest in dealing. Without further thought, he tied up his lines and climbed down over the wheel. There, for the first time, he was made to know a smidgen of shame for his bare feet and patched canvas pants. He felt his face and neck hotten up above the worn homespun shirt as two girls in dainty, ruffled dresses openly snickered at him before going on up the street. The way they were whispering gleeful opinions to each other made it right down unsettling.

It was only when stubborn determination forced his lagging feet into the store that he felt a renewed surge of assurance.

There were a number of shoppers scattered about the place, but none of them seemed to pay him any particular attention. That made him feel more easy-like. And the mixed odors of spices, oiled harness, new clothing, and bulk groceries blended themselves into a web of enchantment that curtained him off from the surrounding world. By the time the younger Mr. Brunner came to wait on him, after reluctantly pulling himself away from the group of men around the hardware counter, his old sense of independence had begun to reassert itself. It was like Pa always claimed: having something worthwhile to dicker with made one man as hefty as another, when it came down to doing business.

And he immediately found he had something worthwhile to dicker with. Vegetables and fresh butter were always in demand in the new settlement, where everyone's attention was centered on digging for gold. Mr. Brunner lost no time in offering to take the whole load at a price considerably above what Rance had expected. It was plumb pleasurable to trade with such a man, especially when he didn't let his store clothes and barbered haircut interfere with his acting just like another anybody.

When Rance drove his wagon to an uncleared lot a hundred yards back of the store, an hour later, he was hard put to keep his eyes off the wealth he had acquired. Flour, cornmeal, sugar, salt, coffee, and a whole caddy of odds and ends that would make for right tasty eating during the winter was a prideful thing to lay eyes on. The bundle of steel traps would set him up to carry out Pa's idea of a fur harvest during the winter, when the farm work left naught else to do. Also, the can of FFFG rifle powder and bars of bullet lead for Pa's old Hawken rifle would be a pretty good guarantee that he could enjoy the whole of it. And now, outfitted with the new shoes and warm store pants he had picked out, he guessed he had about everything any right-minded body could ask for. The fact that the coat Ma had set her heart to was nowhere in sight made the whole thing easier. He didn't know if he could have made it through, faced by the coat hanging there like it was that other time.

Another thing he felt a whole lot grateful for was that Brunner had been too busy talking Indians with the other men to bother asking questions about the Hardigs. It wasn't that he had anything to feel shameful about going ahead on his own after Pa and Ma were killed. That could happen to anybody.

But it wasn't a thing that could be helped by talking about it, now that it was all over. And he didn't want to show up as hunting pity for himself. Moreover, he had no relish for a passel of old-woman gab, should they know he had no folks with him while a few hostiles were acting up. A scad of people were mighty odd-like that way.

The Indian scare, as he had gathered from the men's talk didn't sound like it amounted to much. Somebody, it seemed, had seen a few painted bucks roaming around and figured they were in for an uprising, like they usually did. It was a sort of habit with too many folks. Pa always held that had the Devil been made up like an Indian, the churches would all be full.

"Chances are," he assured himself, "ever'body sighted the same bunch in diff'rent places, 'thout knowin' they all wound up in that stump hole back of my cabin. Be a right tidy joke, was they to know the truth of it. Yet it'd be plumb too bad to pull the props out from under all their hoorawin'."

Well satisfied with his reasoning, he grinned to himself while going silently about cooking a generous supper over his tiny fire. Later, he strolled up the street in the warm darkness. The friendly glow of lighted windows seemed like so many gigantic fireflies scattered over the flat stretching out from the foot of the encircling hills. Rance felt his chest tighten over a sudden strange surge of loneliness. Thinking of all those houses filled with happy families and cheerful voices brought back that first awful day when he was left alone in the empty cabin. However, as Pa always said, even bad soup couldn't be bettered by crying into it. He squared his shoulders abruptly, heading across the street toward a brightly lighted building on the next corner.

The store, or whatever kind of place it was, seemed to be right busy. A scad of folks were going in and out, late as it was. The sight gave him an urge to be among people for a spell; it might help him to shuck off that lonesome feeling a mite. And now that he was rigged out in his new pants and shoes, they likely wouldn't pay him no mind if he just walked in like anybody else.

He paused in front of the place, trying to make out the rest of the indistinct lettering, "–ley Saloo–," thrown into the shadow by a fancy lantern hanging over the door. He pulled at his forelock. Too bad he hadn't come over earlier, while it was light enough to see better. Still, he guessed it didn't matter much what the name was. The hum of voices coming from inside sounded like everybody was plenty sociable. He half turned toward the door just as two men, leading a packhorse, rode up to the hitchrack.

The wilderness instinct to see before being seen pulled Rance a step back into the shadows. His glance flashed over the loaded packhorse. A pick and two shovel handles stuck out from under the flattened bedrolls covering the pack. The dim light couldn't disguise the tattered and begrimed pair who stepped down to tie their horses and clump booted feet across the boardwalk. Prospectors! Rance nodded in the darkness. And apparently in from a long stretch in the hills. He trailed the two in through the swinging door.

Half a dozen voices answered the newcomers' shouted greeting. Red Whiskers threw his hat in the air and yelled for a drink. He licked thick red lips while his beady little eyes ran ferretlike along the bar. His hatchet-faced partner jumped up on a chair, his thin crooked mouth expanding in a broken-toothed grin that belied the coldness of his fishlike eyes.

"Hear you'uns been havin' a gout uh Injun trouble lately," he announced above the suddenly quieted noise. "Redskins sneakin' through the hills all about. Well, there's three uh the yaller bellies we took off yore hands." He reached a bloodstained hand into his shirt front to pull out a trio of black braids from which dangled that many fresh scalps. "We got 'em, Red an' me, jest this afternoon. Too bad the buck got away, but we cut down the kid an' two squaws which is 'bout as good, the way they keep the country flooded with blood-suckin' pups."

He swung the scalps around his head as a chorus of approval ran through the crowd.

Rance was edging his way out the door. He wished he had known the building was a drinking place, before he trailed the men inside. Ma would think unkindly of him, was she to know he had even showed his face in such a place.

Again concealed by the sheltering dark, he hurried back toward his camp. Somewhere in the last few minutes he had lost all desire for companionship. He found himself wondering if the loud-mouthed crowd carried their bawdy language and sour smell of spilled liquor back to the softly lighted homes that had stirred his lonesomeness? He shook his head. There was something about it that didn't fit. Maybe Pa was right in his notion that bunching too many people together sort of spawned some kind of rot, like dumping a lot of fresh meat down in a heap, where each piece lay against another and no air could get into the pile.

An errant thought suggested that Red Whiskers and Hatchet Face would start the rot sprouting in just about anything. He scowled into the darkness. It was funny how a body's mind would toss out ideas sometimes, when he wasn't nowise really thinking. And it seemed like the unharnessed thoughts often had a truer slant on some things than would come by a heap of studying.

At any rate, that pair were sure enough mighty dismal characters, even for prospectors. No rightful man would go around showing a woman's private parts and fresh scalps that way, even if it was from Indians that needed killing. Pa always held a distrust for anybody that would act boastful about killing women and kids, much less mutilate them afterward. Not that Pa was anyways soft in his thinking about redskins; he just figured it was mighty belittling in a man to pick his spite on females of any kind. Looking back on it, Rance was glad he noticed how a lot of men in the saloon had not joined in cheering the prospectors. These looked kind of disgusted and sour-faced instead, as though they maybe misdoubted such sorry goings-on. It made him think they would like as not be eyeing things through the same knothole Pa favored.

Still, the thing fretted him. It was hard to tell just what was right. The sneaking Indians didn't hold off killing white women and youngsters, according to the talk he'd heard. And it had been that way when they murdered his own folks. A sudden surge of hatred pulled his stomach up in a knot. It sure looked like Pa's Bible book had the right of it, where it told about an eye for an eye and a tooth for a tooth. However, that didn't necessarily hold for cutting parts off the squaws, just to make sport. That wasn't nowise the way of civilized folks.

Murky daylight found him still pondering the pros and cons of the matter. It was all very confusing. He squinted up at the leaden, overcast sky. The stir of a southwest wind against his cheek warned him that the quicker he got home, the better it would be for his load of supplies. He dumped a can of water on the coals of his breakfast fire and threw the harness on his team. He guessed he'd best not squander time on fretting about Indians till he got home.

Yet it was hard to mislay thoughts about the Rogues' unprovoked attack on Pa and Ma. Then the scene was brought back to mind with new force a couple of hours later.

He was coming up a long coulee between broken ridges when he pulled his team up sharply behind a vine maple thicket. His eyes had caught the flicker of movement beyond a low gap in the hills. Carefully, he studied the file of moving figures. Indians! There was no misdoubting what they were. And all of a dozen of them. If there hadn't been so many, he almost wished they would come within shooting distance. But they seemed to be heading off to the southwest. Going in that direction would take them well adrift of his place. He didn't know whether to be glad or sorry.

CHAPTER 4

The steady pounding of rain on the roof was in Rance's ears when he stirred himself awake. It had been raining all night. Dim gray light filtered in through the piece of raw deerhide he had fastened over the square window hole, allowing it to dry and shrink itself into opaque thinness.

"I'm proud to know I got that fixed up while it was warm an' dry enough to fashion a proper job," he mused. "Doin' things at the right time, as Pa allus held, shore saves a heap of regretfulness later on."

He eyed the buckskin thongs he had contrived for operating the outside wooden shutter, hinged at the top. By merely adjusting the thongs, it was a simple matter to raise the shutter for a maximum of light, lower it as a slanted cover for the deerskin covering in stormy weather, or close it entirely for warmth and comfort. And all without setting a foot outside. He hoped Pa could see how it worked, from up there wherever he was. Pa took a heap of pride in folks who could skirmish out better ways of doing things.

The more he thought about his creation, the better he felt. A tight-shut cabin could get mighty wearisome when a rainfall liken this one took a notion to hang on for a spell. As it was, the half-raised shutter gave him light enough to make out with a leisurely breakfast, while the water cascaded off the sloping boards without even dampening the hide window covering. Come night, he could drop it shut with a quick twist of the wrist and hole up snug as a bear in its den.

Slopping out to the barn to feed the stock and milk old Brockle, he felt a smidgen of pride in his decision to make the trip out to Jacksonville while the weather was still holding fair. There was no telling when the trail would be fit to travel again. As it was, having all his winter's supplies safely inside the cabin ahead of the rainy season was a thing to lift a body's feelings. Along with having his roothouse filled to the muzzle and the stock feed under cover, he guessed he about had the world by the tail with a downhill pull. His shrill whistle speared through the rain's dull hammering without missing a note of "Oh! Susanna."

He put in the rest of the forenoon securing his stock of goods against possible damage from mice and dampness. The homemade bins of rived cedar slabs was good enough for everyday use, but the row of bags hung from the ridgepole promised safe storage for the bulk of things to be held more or less indefinitely.

Rance ran a satisfied glance around the room as he made a hasty meal of breakfast leftovers. He had put his bullet mold and lead dipper to heat in front of the fireplace. It seemed like a fitting afternoon for making up a supply of bullets. While he might not need an overload of rifle balls for a space of time, it gave a healthful feeling to have plenty on hand. A body never knew what might come up. Anyhow, there was no calculating when he would have another real housed-in day like this to spend on casting bullets. These early storms didn't usually run much to length.

This storm, however, seemed bred to a contrary nature. Shortly before dark, the rain changed to a stinging, icy sleet. When he came in from doing his barn chores, the wind was driving frozen pellets under the half-raised window shutter to rattle against dried rawhide. Rance hurriedly butted the door shut and lowered the window shutter. It felt mighty soothful to hear the latch slip into place and outside sounds dissolve into drowsy quietness. He threw a couple of pine knots onto the fire. It was mighty restful to watch their flare chase the shadows back into the corners of the room. A warm blanket of comfort and security draped itself around him. Here was everything a body could ask for, except family companionship. He felt that old familiar lump arise in his throat. Blank loneliness clouded his vision for a moment. But no, it wasn't seemly to tarry on such thoughts. He shook his shoulders brusquely. Pa always held that lowering oneself to fault the Lord's manner of doing things was only the way of sorry weaklings and no-accounts. A full man stood up to the hurtful tests God set in his path, being thankful he was still able to climb over these rough spots.

He rubbed a hard hand across his eyes. "I don't reckon," he muttered to himself, "that Pa an' Ma would be anyways pleasured at me mushin' down under the dismals, instead of humpin' my spine inta the chores they hadn't time to finish."

There was a saying, mayhaps in Pa's Bible book, about how a mind busy with peerin' ahead, or upward, took the heft of the load off of an overly burdened heart. That made a lot of sense, come to study on it. The main thing was try to remember it when he felt himself walking into a cloud.

His wandering glance fell on the trimmings from his new rifle balls, scattered over the fireplace hearth. One hand instinctively reached for the brush broom behind the door, his detached mind half-consciously speculating on the number of balls or shotgun slugs these sweepings would make. No sensible body let such needful things go to waste.

And it was surprising how much better the hearth looked,

with all the ashes and dirt swept into the fire. It made his cluttered table show up right shameful. And the disordered bedroom, that stood as Ma had left it midway of a busy day, was no better. It was a sorry sort of a person, he decided, who would neglect a rightful job liken that for so long, especially when its doing wouldn't take but a few minutes.

By the time he had tidied up both rooms, he had made up his mind that he might as well take the bedroom for his own use. Backed up against the hollowed-out wooden dish trough, listening to the dishwater gurgle out through the hollow elderberry limb that Pa had fixed to drain the water out through the wall, he could see no rightful need for him to bed down in the leanto shed, now that he had the whole house to himself. It was funny such an idea hadn't come to life before. Mayhaps that was what happened to a body who never had time to think. His eyes traveled slowly around the room, taking in the meager furnishings. One hand strayed to his forelock. He guessed he had done everything but take another look at the weather before going to bed.

He opened the door to a silent world. The sleet-coated bushes stood ghostly in the light from the open door. Tree trunks were coated with ice a half-inch thick and tiny twigs had grown to the size of pitchfork handles. Now that the wind had gone down, the quiet darkness seemed to have warmed up considerable. Rance felt a featherlike flake of moisture settle on his nose. He held out one hand. A moment later, he made out the white snowflake nestled in his palm. Then several more drifted down in front of his eyes. He sniffed the air. The lowering sky promised a white blanket spread over the country before morning.

"That would fix it for a likely chance to scout out a deer," he reasoned. "A good snow cover'd let a body sneak through the woods 'thout nary a bit of soundin' off. And it's time I was lookin' to my winter's meat." He glanced up to assess the rapidly thickening cloud of white flakes. "Yes, sir, I reckon this is purely made to order. It 'pears I was prodded inta makin' them extra rifle balls just in time."

He stepped back inside and dropped the oak bar across the door. Going deer hunting was a prime thing to favor a night's sleep. He slanted a glance at the Hawken rifle before blowing out his bedside candle.

The storm, however, seemed in no hurry to further his plan. When he lifted the window shutter to a murky dawn, he saw only a tumbling cloud of snow drifting down between the window and the nearest trees. Three or four inches of the stuff already covered the ground. The way it was coming down, it would be shin-deep by night. He turned back to rake the ashes from the bed of live coals, the thought of breakfast crowding into his mind.

"Let 'er snow!" he grunted optimistically. "The more comes, the better the huntin'll be. Trackin' should be good, if the deer ain't all bunched up in the thickets."

He lifted to his feet and stepped over to the shelf cupboard for the cornmeal jar. With his hand halfway into the stone jar, his eyes met the accusing stare of the nearly empty candle box. He tipped the box half over to make sure of the count. Yes, only seven left! Another pesky chore he had put off almost too long. Well, mayhaps this stormy day was made to force his hand. It seemed like finding himself house-bound was the only way some things ever got done.

He stirred cornmeal slowly into the small iron mush pot, his mind on the candle box. Later, he rummaged Ma's candlemold and cake of candle tallow out of the old Missouri oak chest, dedicated to the storage of occasionals. He hoped Ma had mixed the needful amount of alum with the tallow. Otherwise, they'd just have to be on the weak side. Alum was one thing he had not thought to get in town. He rummaged further for the melting pot Pa had made out of an old syrup can, cut off above the pouring spout. With his equipment assembled on one end of the split-log table, he swung the mush pot and coffee back from the main heat of the fire while he went out to milk and feed the stock.

"Have plenty of time to make a scad of candles after I eat," he assured himself. "Got the heft of the day for it, unless this storm tapers off mighty sudden." He slanted a weather eye up at the snow-filled sky. "And I don't reckon it'll do much taperin' off anyways immediate."

Nor was he mistaken. The snow continued to pile up on the doorstep in time with the rapidly filling candle box. This last Rance estimated to be a full winter's supply. He balanced the last candle on top of the pyramided mound to find he still had half the afternoon to tidy up the cabin before choretime. He guessed the Lord knew a body needed a good storm in order to get at all the odd jobs around the house.

"Should it last over tomorrow," he thought, "I'll mayhaps git that two weeks' butter making caught up, an' suds out my dirty clo'es."

But the weather was kind enough to push these extra tasks aside in an obliging manner. By the time Rance finished his breakfast and outdoor chores, the storm had thinned out to scattered flakes. He studied the overcast sky thoughtfully. Though clearing somewhat, a heavy bank of clouds was building up in the southwest. More snow by nightfall, if all signs held out. Mayhaps sooner! But there should be a fair easing off for a sizable chunk of the day, enough for him to slip out and collect a deer or two. A little extra meat would be a handsome backlog for his food bins, should this weather turn into an old he-goat of a storm that penned him in for a spell.

"Accordin' to what some of the early-comers told Pa about that waist-deep snowfall up in these hills, a few years back, a body might git tol'able meat hungry, was it to come again." Rance twisted his straw-colored forelock into a spiral while his eyes inspected the sky a second time. "Yep, I reckon's how I'd best take this slackenin' spell for a look-see. It might git bad, was it to set in agin."

He went back into the cabin and heaped a mound of ashes over his breakfast fire. Turning, his gaze rested for a long moment on the new store pants. He shook his head regretfully. No telling what kind of a bloody mess a body might run into before he got a deer dressed out and packed home. Anyhow, he'd keep warm enough in these canvas pants and Pa's old mackinaw. He slung the powder horn over one shoulder and dropped a handful of the new rifle balls into the poke at his waist. Tucking the Hawken rifle under his arm, he carefully fastened the cabin door on his way out to saddle the gray mare.

Rance guessed it to be crowding ten o'clock, judging by the lighter spot in the clouds which covered the sun when he rode up the creek. Time, however, wasn't a thing to waste much thought on. Most of his attention centered itself on the scattered fir thickets dotting the coulee that led south away from the creek. Pa always claimed that deer held more wisdom than most humans, being crafty enough to shelter up in comfort, when the weather was unlikely, instead of barging around just to show how tough they were.

From the absence of tracks or any visible movement, it began to look like the deer were overly set on comfort this morning. Or mayhaps they were wise enough to hyper down into the lower country before the storm. They were pretty smart critters. At any rate, an hour's riding from thicket to thicket disclosed no sign of life. The animals were either stubbornly clinging to their beds under the slim white tepees of snow-caked boughs or had moved elsewhere. Rance knew that forcing his way into the clumps of half-grown firs would settle the question, but thoughts of all that snow tumbling down his neck rose to override such an approach. As a last resort, perhaps, but the day was still young. There was no profit in letting overhurry push him into a soaking. He rode on.

He let the gray mare pick her own way through a series of brushy hollows and across intervening ridges. It was all the same. A haze-covered bright spot in the southern sky warned him it was in the neighborhood of high noon when he finally saw his first deer. It was sneaking out of some hillside brush when he slid down from the gray mare to settle his sights on the blue-gray shoulder. Echoes of the rifle's sharp crack rode the single wild leap of the buck.

"Meat in the pot!" Rance grinned his satisfaction, seeing no further movement. "Right sizable, too. Worth comin' a fair stretch for."

He hurried the gray mare up the slope and set about hog-dressing the animal. It was a prime buck, well fleshed and larded with fat. He grunted his pleasure at its extra-large size as he wrestled the carcass onto the mare's back, behind the saddle. He guessed his meat problem was solved for a reasonable spell, not to mention all that tallow-grease for soap-making. Yes, it had been a good day.

The next thing was to get it home before the storm blew in. He sighted out his bearings. The hunt had led him in a circuitous route around to the east and then southwesterly. There was no use in backtracking all that way. The simplest way would be to head straight north toward that narrow gap in the hills. This should bring him out somewhere on that big flat a few miles west of the home creek. There, if he wasn't off on his calculations, he could cut straight across to the cabin. Three hours, maybe, allowing for the extra load on the horse.

Unfortunately, it wasn't to be all that simple. Fate seemed jealously determined to relinquish none of the powers with which she had been governing the Hardig affairs.

Rance's lazy whistle was droning through "Oh! Susanna" when he topped out on a low ridge. The tune died abruptly as he sucked in a sharp breath. Blank surprise widened his eyes. A thin spiral of smoke was drifting skyward beyond a fringe of trees half a mile ahead. He reached up to tug at his forelock. Who would be making a smoke out here in the middle of nowhere, where nobody should rightfully be at this time of year?

He urged the gray mare cautiously forward. A quick glance assured him he had not forgotten to recap the long rifle resting across his thighs. He was careful to keep the bulk of the trees between himself and the smoke, until he could use their shelter to work around for a satisfactory glimpse of what was going on. Pa always held that getting the first look at unknowns was the best life insurance a man could find.

Rance got his look a few minutes later. Scouting around the edge of the thinning timber, he managed to find an opening that framed a corner of the little flat before him. Startled wonder pulled his mouth into a big O at sight of the still smoking remnants of what had been a covered wagon.

CHAPTER 5

"Now, what's a lone wagon doin' way up here?" he asked in wondering breath. "Miles away from any road an' winter sneakin' close. And how come it burnt in all this wet snow? It 'pears to've taken fire right recent, most like whilst 'twas still stormin'."

He rode out into the open, looking for the owners of the outfit. There was, however, no one to be seen. Neither were any horses nor oxen about. He sent a yell ringing through the timber. His only answer was the scolding of a pine squirrel back in the timber to the right. He thumped the gray mare in the ribs, reining her over toward the wagon.

There he came face to face with the whole pitful story. Nobody could be mistaken in what had happened. Rance thought of his loud shout, and felt a cold chill run up his spine. Anxious eyes searching the semicircle of timber, he rode slowly around the grisly heap of charred ruins, looking like some hideous island set amidst a peaceful ocean of unsullied white. A thin line of horse tracks led off through the snow to the west. A few half-obliterated moccasin tracks were still visible on the lee side of where the smoking wagon stood. The lower leg of a man, still encased in its fire-warped boot, protruded from the central heap of ashes. A few charred bits of harness, a couple of smoke-blackened kettles, a wad of bed quilts, still sending up their thin spiral of smoke, told him all he needed to know.

Rance felt his stomach jerk convulsively. The sight seemed to blend in with a last memory of his parents. The same old story!

"Damn the murderin' redskins! Damn all Injuns! They're worse than so many wolves slaverin' with hydrophobia. I wish —I wish—"

Whatever he wished was lost under a faint cry from back in the timber. He threw up his head, listening intently. His mind had suddenly emptied itself of everything else. The gray mare pawed nervously with a restless hoof. He jerked her back to quietness. Then he heard the faint voice again. It seemed to be coming from off to the right.

"Either middlin' far off or weakened down a sight," he concluded. "Mayhaps one got away, only partly killed."

This last possibility appeared most likely. He had heard of scalped people coming back to life, or partly so, after being left for dead. He swung the mare around toward the timber.

Yet he moved cautiously, the cocked rifle in his hands. Indians had a trick of decoying folks into a trap, like a body would use a clipped-wing goose to call other unsuspecting birds down to a pond.

He reined the mare in slower, eyes and ears hair-triggered for any off note or movement. Only the rackety pounding of a woodpecker broke the stillness. It was coming from the direction of the voice, a fairish indication that no bunch of redskins was prowling around in that quarter. He urged the mare on.

He was almost up to the outer fringe of timber when he saw a woman floundering through the snow in his direction. At first, he thought it was an old, white-headed lady, then closer approach disclosed strands of dark hair peeping through the plaster of snow. She looked like she had been wallowing in the stuff. A mixture of dry twigs and wet snow clung in blotches all over her dress and light jacket.

Rance slid from the mare and hurried to meet her. Best not let her get out of the trees, where she could fairly sight the burnt wagon. It was nothing for a woman's eyes, even though it was her own outfit. He tried to stay between her and the smoking debris as she almost fell into his arms.

"Oh—oh, thank God!" The voice was a choking sob. "You found me. A white man!"

"Yes, you're safe, ma'am. I'll take keer of you." He slid one hand under her chin to lift the tortured white face. "Don't you fret yourself none—" He broke off in confusion, pulling his hand away. His mouth sagged half open. "Why, why, you're just a girl!" he managed weakly.

"Can I help that?" Her words came in a hoarse whisper above the labored breathing. "The Indians killed all the others while I was after wood. I'm all that's left." A spasm of sobs shook the thin shoulders pressed against his chest.

"I wasn't nowise castin' blame, ma'am." He patted her back awkwardly. "Surprise, mostly, backfired my spoken words. Now, the main thing is to git you home an' thawed out. You've had a time! There's nary thing we kin do here. And the day's dwindlin'."

"Is it far?"

"A fair piece." He paused for a glance around the little flat. "Injuns took your horses, I reckon?"

"I—I g-guess so. I kind of lost track of—"

The one swift glance past his shoulder brought a stifled cry, half smothered by the hand clapped suddenly over her mouth.

"No matter! You kin ride the gray mare." He pulled her abruptly around and lifted her into the saddle. "We'll make out."

She made no protest. Her eyes stared blankly ahead.

"It 'pears you'll have to make out with that dress as it is," he said, wiping a streak of snow where her full skirt had swiped across his face in mounting. "It's chillin' wet, but I've got nothin' to better it. But," he was pulling off his worn mackinaw, "this'll mayhaps let a little warmishness build up 'ginst the rest of you. That skimpy little jacket you've got on might help keep your wet head an' face from freezin'."

"But I can't take your coat. You'll suf—"

"Won't neither! I'll keep plenty hot walkin' in this snow. You don't fret about me."

She was too weary and dispirited to argue. He buttoned the coat around her in silence. She twisted the jacket about her head and neck. It did feel good, or would as soon as she built up some body heat under it.

Rance picked up the gray mare's reins and started to move ahead, only to stop in midstride.

"Hey, wait a minute!"

A wayward drift of smoke from the burning quilts had struck his nostrils with a helpful suggestion. Maybe they weren't all gone! He turned his back on the girl to shuffle hurriedly through the snow to the wagon remains. There, shielding his nose from the sickening odor of burnt flesh, one clawing hand found the edge of a cotton-filled comforter still only smoldering. It burst into flame when he jerked it free, throwing it to one side, but he quickly tramped the blaze out in the snow. Both ends were still fairly whole. They would help. He returned to the horse, dragging them behind him. It took but a moment to wrap the blackened pieces around the girl's legs, tucking the ends securely between the stirrup straps.

"Sorta dampish," he said, "but they'll keep the wind out. And they'll warm up some—I hope."

They moved out without saying anything more, Rance leading the mare. He figured he'd better save his breath for the work ahead, while the girl was too woebegone to do more than sway woodenly in the saddle. It was easy to see that she was about at the end of her rope. Fright, grief, and weariness, along with the chill from hours in a snowbank, demanded that he get her to the cabin as soon as possible. Going back the roundabout way he had come meant extra distance. It was too big a risk. He turned his eyes directly north. Holding his course on that high granite ridge would, he believed, bring them out on the creek somewhere above the cabin. He eyed the heavier bank of clouds swiftly building up in the southwest. It had already shut off the sun's weak effort to break through the overcast. They didn't have too much time. He hoped the light would last until he reached more familiar ground. A big snowfall like this really made an oddment of things. It gave him sort of a puckerish feeling to be uncertain about even the spots vaguely remembered from the one time he had escaped work to come up here for a short hunt. Still, he reckoned he'd make out all right. Pa always held that a man who set his sights and kept his head wasn't apt to run overly wide of his mark.

He plodded on. From time to time, his thoughts picked up a picture of the girl he had rescued. Right pretty, she would be, if she wasn't so scared and beat out and loaded down with miseries. That almost black hair looked to have a sight of curl in it, where it fanned out around her pinched face. And the soft, brown eyes, remindful of a shot doe waiting to have its throat cut, would light up her whole face, once she got minded to shape up a smile. He recalled the skimpy weight of her body, when he put her on the mare, and the way her heart pounded against his chest. It seemed like she was laboring to breathe. Could she be running afoul of a bad cold? That wouldn't be surprising, after being bushed up such a while in the snow. And scheming to hide her clothes by plastering them with more snow hadn't been any help. The whole thing was enough to give a body lung fever. He hoped Ma hadn't misspoken herself that time old Brockle like to've died from eating poison weeds, and she explained how God usually had an eye out for stricken critters. It was a comforting thought.

But comforting thoughts have a way of deserting when trouble closes ranks for a fresh assault. Rance's legs began to feel like wooden sticks, after the first hour, while his rifle had doubled in weight. He fished a leather thong out of his pocket and stopped to sling the gun on the saddle horn. That helped for a while. Then he caught the sound of muffled sobbing from the hunched figure behind him. The distressed weeping, only half audible through compressed lips, flooded him with a sense of helpless frustration that doubled his weariness. He felt the harshness of a scolding rebuke rise in his throat. Wasn't he doing the best he could to help her? And didn't he have plenty of troubles of his own? But he choked the words back in time. Bellering about it wouldn't help a great sight. And she did have her miseries. He half turned to say something comforting, when his dragging feet tripped over a hidden rock. The next instant, arms flailing, he sprawled full length in the snow.

For a moment, he lay still. The snow felt so restful. Aching muscles protested any further exertion. It was the girl's sharp cry that stirred him to movement. He shook his head and lurched to his knees. Had to get her to the cabin! She'd freeze out here. Brushing the snow from his clothing with one hand, he pushed to his feet. He half wished he were a girl, so he could cry, too. He turned slowly, looking for his landmark. The granite ridge was only a darker shadow in the gloom that seemed to have suddenly thickened in the last few moments. His swift upward glance met a heavier mass of lowering overcast. He felt a cold raw breeze fan against his cheek. Then it began to snow, thick, smothering flakes that shut off vision at a dozen rods.

He had one last glimpse of the ridge before the storm closed down in a murky white veil of wind-driven snow. They must be somewhat over halfway home, he thought, trying to bolster his lagging energy. And he should be able to hold his direction by keeping the wind on his left cheek. He headed down the slope toward the scattered timber dotting a rather wide bench. The trees would help some, if he didn't run into a mess of woolly brush farther down.

"How much farther?" asked the halting voice behind him. "I am freezing to death!"

"Pound yourself with your hands. Swing your arms. Anything to keep up circulation. It won't be long." He didn't look back.

An early darkness was adding its weight to the swirling snow, when they came down off the bench. The last quarter mile had been a sliding scramble. Rance was no longer sure of how well he had kept his directions since night set in. Suppose he had wandered off his course? Suppose the wind had shifted? The thought brought a hollow emptiness to the pit of his stomach. Such a mistake would be well nigh fatal. He pulled at his forelock. There didn't seem much a body could do about it now.

But wait! His mind stirred sluggishly. Hadn't Pa once said something about horses always being able to find their way home, day or night? Hm-m-m! It was worth a trial. He looped the reins over the saddle horn and walked around to grab the gray mare by the tail. At least, being pulled along would be a sight easier than having to break a trail.

The mare seemed willing. She led out at once, bearing

somewhat more to the left from the course he had been taking. Rance stumbled along in her wake. He had almost stopped thinking.

It was some thirty minutes later that he came back to full realization with a start. His feet were no longer blundering over uneven ground. And the mare had hurried her pace. He shook himself into a semblance of alertness. They were on some kind of a trail, a broken trail. And who but he had been around to break a track since last night's snow? His head came up with a jerk. Why, the creek trail, of course, where he had gone out that morning. The sudden awareness of accomplishment sent his eyes sweeping from left to right. That downed log with its three-prong limb almost brought a shout to his lips. Farther on appeared the big boulder, undercut on the trail side to show its red-striped face above the snow. Why, he was only half a mile from home!

Rance felt the tug of the gray mare's tail as she instinctively quickened her gait. The blinding snow abruptly lost most of its oppressive threat. Thought of the snug cabin ahead lengthened his stride. Sheer relief bubbled in his throat. He didn't know whether he was fixing to laugh or cry.

And the cabin held all its protective warmth, when he shoved open the door. He was trying to help the half-frozen girl from the horse when both of them went sprawling in the snow. They sat staring at each other for a moment.

"This is it," he said inanely, collecting his wits enough to scramble to his feet and half carry her into the cabin. "Nothin' much to fret about now." He set her down in the cherrywood rocker, then dropped to his knees in front of the fireplace. "Have a fire right smart now."

He raked away the heavy covering of ashes with stiffened fingers, his hands hovering there a moment to savor the live coals winking up at him. His strong breath was loaded with a sigh of relief as the handful of pine splinters burst into immediate flame. Carefully, he tepeed a circle of split kindling around the blaze before reaching for a candle. The warm smoke caressed his hands and face like a benediction. He filled the extra iron kettle with water and hung it beside the stew pot on the fireplace crane. Centering both kettles over the fire, he stacked a rick of heavier wood over and around the leaping flames.

"Have you thawed out good in a few minutes now." He canted a glance at the white face, her eyes seemingly frozen in an unwinking stare. "Hey, you're all right, ain't you?"

"Y-yes."

"Good! Have things hotted up in no time. You just relax an' get outa them wet duds as quick—"

He caught himself just in time. He could almost hear Ma chide him for such an unseemly way of talking to a girl.

"I'll find you some of Ma's things. You kin shift clo'es whilst I put up the mare an' milk Brockle. 'Fore I git back, you kin be swaddled up in a dry outfit. 'Twill make you fittin' to git some pure good outa this heat. Then some of this stew an' a mug of coffee'll put new life inta both of us."

He went into the bedroom and rummaged behind the curtain in the clothes-hanging corner. Pa's suit of carefully darned underwear would be best for real body warmth, he decided. Wool was fine to quicken the blood, and it wouldn't be a thing to notice under one of Ma's long nightgowns. Some long stockings and a pair of moccasins would rig her up first rate. Then she wouldn't have to do anything but shed the moccasins when she readied for bed.

He dropped the clothes on the bench before the fire. "You change now, whilst I tend the stock. Gotta git yourself shet of them freezin' things 'thout tarryin'."

She still sat immovable, staring at nothing. He reached over to shake her roughly.

"You hear me? You git changed whilst I'm out doin' for the stock!"

"Y-yes, I guess so." Her hoarse voice seemed to be coming from a long distance.

"No guessin' about it! You gotta do it, you wanta live! Or will I have to handle the job?"

"No, I'll manage. Just so—so tired. It's hard to move."

He lifted her to her feet and pulled the soggy mackinaw from her shoulders. "Then git busy! You'll feel better, once you're dry. I reckon to find you all fixed up agin I finish the barn chores. Understand?"

"Yes, I do—I will." His hard hands and rough voice had brought a show of life to her face. "But don't be long. It's fearsome to be alone." Her shoulders twitched sharply under his fingers.

"There's naught to harm you here. And I'll hurry smart as I kin. 'Twill take only a few minutes to milk an' feed. So you don't do any dallyin' either."

She nodded. He saw she was fumbling with the buttons of her blouse as he went out the door. Still in some'at of a daze, he reckoned, but his words looked to've taken holt. It seemed now she was fixing to make out all right. Cold had a way of sometimes doing oddments to people, left to themselves. He was glad he had been a mite rough with her.

And she did look better, when he came in with his bucket of milk. The underwear had disappeared beneath the nightgown. She had pulled her chair closer to the heat. Her own clothes were piled in a sodden heap at the end of the fireplace.

"Good girl!" Rance nodded approvingly. "Now a bait of this fresh milk an' a morsel of hot stew to waken your innards. I hope that fire is dreenin' off your worst chill."

"The worst of it," she admitted croakingly. "It feels so good to be halfway warm again. And safe inside four walls." She snugged the nightgown closer around her.

Rance set the bucket down to reach for a setting pan. The tail of his eye caught a shiver under the bulky gown. He immediately stepped back to pull the kettle off the crane. His other hand reached for the wooden foot tub upended beside the occasional chest. He poured the tub half full of the hot water, then put the kettle back where it would stay hot.

"Nothin' like a good foot soakin' to head off a risin' cold." He moved the tub across to her chair and then turned back to his unstrained milk. "You peel your stockings an' git your feet inta that water!" he said over his shoulder. "Be the best thing for you. If it's too hot, I'll temper it down some."

Faint rustlings behind him, followed by a sharp exclamation, told him his orders were in effect. He reached for a gourd of cold water, turning to see a pair of reddened feet held above the tub. He grinned shyly as he poured a second gourdful, then tested the water with his finger.

"Be all right now." He rose to his feet. "You kin go on with your soakin' whilst I git inta some dry clo'es. Then I'll fix us something to eat."

He paused, half turning, on his way to the bedroom. "The gourd's there handy," he said. "You keep addin' a mite of that hot water every little bit, as the tub cools. I'll be right back."

Rance was wearing his new store pants and shoes, when he came out of the bedroom a few minutes later. He shrugged luxuriously inside the new garments as he tossed his wet things down beside hers. Time enough to hang them up for a good dryout after they had eaten. He crossed on over to the shelf cupboard and took down the pair of wooden bowls carved from maple burls. Ma, he guessed, would allow this was a special enough occasion for using the birthday gift Pa had made for her. He ran a finger gently across the raised initials carved beneath the bowls' rims. The move brought that old lump crawling up into his throat. He turned hurriedly to start ladling the steaming stew from the pot.

The girl took one of the filled bowls from his hand. "You are here alone?" Her words blurred through the mixture of meat and vegetables.

"Alone, yes."

"Where are your people?"

"Same as yourn; Injuns bushwhacked 'em two months agone."

"Oh!" She sucked in her breath, half strangling on the thick soup. "I'm sorry!"

"There's naught for you to fret about. You couldn't know."

"But I'm still sorry, sorry for anybody whose folks fell afoul of the red murderers."

"Mine went quick. They didn't have to suffer any miserables."

"So did mine. They went down all at once, when the savages—there must have been a full dozen of them—jumped out of that gully to start shooting. Father, Mother, and little Johnny were caught flat-footed. I was back in the timber, hunting dry wood. I heard them screeching, but by the time I got out to where I could see what was happening, they had piled the bodies in the wagon and set it afire. All I could do was run and hide."

"What time this morning did it happen?" Rance's mind recalled the Rogues he had seen heading south on his return from town. "And you say there were a dozen of them?"

"Something like that. I was too scared to do close counting. It was early this morning, shortly after it quit snowing." Memory twisted her face into a mask of agony. "It was so—so h-horrible!" she sobbed brokenly. "The filthy, murdering scum!"

"How come you folks were up in this tangle of hills, all alone, 'thout no comp'ny an' nary a road?"

"Plain lost, we were." She looked up, seemingly glad to find the talk veering away from the killings. "It was the climax of all our summer's troubles. The Illinois train we were with from Independence never cottoned to us Tennesseans. When we had to stop for Mother's sickness, this side of Fort Hall, they plain drove off and left us."

"Where at were these here Illinois scalawags aheadin' for?"

"Somewhere in the Willamette Valley, if you know where that is; a place called French Prairie, I believe they called it."

"You don't reckon they mighta stopped off at the Jacksonville gold diggin's?" A vision of himself overtaking this heartless company and forcibly calling them to account for their almost criminal selfishness flashed through his mind. "Hearing about the new diggin's and its bein' a sight handier than the Willamette could be a right smart mind changer," he added hopefully.

She shook her head. "I doubt that it would change any minds in that company. They belonged to a religious sect which pinned its faith on setting themselves apart in a community devoted to farming. They planned to establish such a colony out here in this new land while they still had unlimited room and little conflict with other settlers. All they could think of was the empire they hoped to build before any interference came about. That was no doubt why they were willing, if not glad, to leave us behind. It is also why I don't believe they would be drawn aside by possibilities of gold, or anything else. At least, not so long as old man Tullock is alive to lead them toward their Promised Land."

"I see!" Rance sat back, all ideas of seeking retribution

abandoned. "But what gets me is the thought of you folks making out by your lonesomes all that way. Specially this late in the season."

"There was nothing else to do, after they abandoned us. We had got off to a late start, then ran into assorted troubles all the way across. Everyone felt winter would catch us if we went north by the Columbia River Trail. They'd told us at Fort Hall about some man by the name of Applegate who had laid out a more southern road to Oregon, so the company voted to go that way."

Memory pulled her face into harsh lines as her voice sank to a whisper. Rance got up to tuck the quilt closer about her, then put fresh wood onto the fire. He sat back down waiting for her to go on.

She straightened herself with a quick shrug, brushing a hand across her eyes. "Well," she continued, "a few days after branching off from the northern trail, Mother got too sick to travel. We simply had to camp until she was able to ride. There was nothing else to do. Meanwhile, the others drove on without us. Left alone, we had no hope of ever catching up. All we could do was follow their wagon tracks. No doubt we would have made it through all right, if this snow hadn't suddenly covered all sight of the trail. Before we realized it, we were completely lost among a jumble of hills that all looked alike. The only thing left for us was to keep going, in hopes of reaching some settlement."

Rance let his breath run out in a long, whistling sigh. "All that, and then run inta this stray bunch of red butchers, where they had no rightly cause to be. And plumb on the home stretch, too. You couldn't have been more'n a day or so's drive off the main trail. It's just purely unreasonable!"

"As unreasonable as your folks getting killed, I suppose, however it happened?"

"Yeah, I reckon, put that way." Rance felt a fresh surge of emptiness climb up his insides. "But dwellin' on the oddments of it ain't goin' to prosper us any. I'd say the best thing we could do is harvest a scad of sleep. We're both nigh tuckered out, an' that freezin' you took sounds like it was clampin' down for a real croupy cold. We kin talk some more later on. Things may perk up agin the sun shows itself."

CHAPTER 6

Rance moved his blankets back to the old pole bunk in the leanto. A woman should have herself a private-like place, and there was only one bedroom. By the time he had the heated doorstep rock wrapped in a discarded shirt and stowed in the foot of her bed, weariness was making him fight to keep his eyes open. He almost forgot to bank the fire before collapsing into the bunk. The hazy question of what he would do with the girl was slugged into oblivion by a sudden wave of unconsciousness, a moment later.

He had no idea what time it might be when he stirred into wakefulness. The cabin was only faintly gray with light. Two red coals stared at him from the fireplace. They looked like the eyes of a drunkard, one half closed and the other canted off slaunchwise. He hurried across the room to raise the window shutter. Even the murky light from outdoors did little to lift the gloom from inside the cabin. Opening the door didn't improve things much. The snow was still piling down in a swirling smother.

"It's truly a prideful thing we made it in last night." He pulled thoughtfully at his forelock. "It looks like I might have a right plenty of time to figger some out for the girl. The trail stands to be snowblocked a'ready, an' she's still amountin'."

He pushed the door shut and built up the fire. A quick surge of well-being stirred in his chest, as the firelight chased lurking shadows out of the room. A body sure had no outs with luck when rightly favored with a snug cabin and plenty of good wood. A new briskness helped him fill the coffeepot and sling the mush kettle on the crane. He dumped the foot tub out the door, then took the dried clothing from the kindling sticks wedged under the fireplace mantel.

Keeping his ears cocked for any sound within the bedroom, he made two slow circuits past the silent door. He built the fire up brighter and swung the crane around out of the direct heat. The same silence greeted another visit to the bedroom door.

"Poor thing!" he decided, "she musta been plumb downright frazzled. Hurt an' cold really pole-axed her. Well-l, sleep's most curin'." He picked up the milk pail and shrugged into his mackinaw. "She might favor my bein' out, anyhow, was she to wake up in a strange-like place."

The bedroom door, however, still frowned forbiddingly when he came in from caring for the stock. One brief glance and he set the bucket down, reaching for the brush broom. He was snow plastered to his waist. It wasn't nowise fitting to drag such a mess into the cabin. He stepped back outside to brush himself off carefully, then moved over to the fireplace. Helped by the brisk blaze, the room had become quite cheerful. He backed up to the fire, feeling the dampish pant legs absorb its welcome warmth. His eyes again drifted across the closed bedroom door. One hand strayed to his forelock.

"Mayhaps I should waken her," he speculated. "She must be gant as a new calf by now. Still, sleep's a bolstering thing for frayed bodies."

He shook his head, turning to ladle out a bowlful of the cornmeal mush. It would probably be no mismove to shy off disturbing her for a spell longer.

Vague uneasiness, however, continued to plague him. Suppose she was bad sick? Suppose something had taken her past ever waking up? He opened the door to peer speculatively into the storm. A faint lightness in the overhead murk suggested that the forenoon was over half gone. It was time that even a beat-up body was stirring about. He swung the crane around to bang it loudly against the fireplace wall. Other exaggerated noises accompanied his fire fixing, skimming the cream off into the tin churn, and washing up the breakfast things.

None of it seemed to have any effect. Nothing sounded from behind the grim bedroom door. Rance pulled at his forelock as he made his way slowly across to the unresponsive door. He laid his ear against the planks, holding his breath intently. Only silence rewarded his effort.

He straightened up, worry etching his forehead. "Hey!" he called, "you awake yet? Oh, miss–miss–" He broke off abruptly, wondering why, in all their talk, he had thought of her as only that Tennessee girl, without ever asking her name. He rapped on the door again, groping for words. "Hey, Miss–Miss Tenny!"

But this brought no better results. He stared at the ceiling for a moment, seeking counsel. Then, his eyes still on the ceiling, he lifted the latch. Carefully shoving the door open a trifle, he paused half bent over as his ears caught the sound of harsh, uneven breathing.

Uncertainty tied his feet to the floor as he shoved the door wider open to look inside. The dim light revealed only a slim mound of patchwork quilts topped by a flushed face and tangle of black curls. Under his gaze, the patchwork mound stirred fretfully, appearing to jerk the pinched face from side to side in a spasm of tortured breathing.

Rance moved hesitantly on into the room. Bashful awkwardness encumbered his feet as he approached closer to the bed. That breathing sounded right down bad! It seemed mighty like that time the little Richards girl all but died of lung fever before Ma doctored her out of it, back there on the Columbia River Trail. He took another step forward to lay his hand on the burning hot forehead.

"Miss—Miss Tenny, are you ailin' as bad as I fear for?" His voice was weighted with apprehensive concern.

A muffled groan was his only answer.

He caught a flash of overbright eyes before she flung her head sidewise in a paroxysm of choked coughing. She rolled half over, her voice a mumble of meaningless words. Rance turned back to the outer room, one hand pushing the beads of sweat up from his forehead. He tugged at the straw-colored lock of hair hanging over one eye. Memory twisted a knot in his insides.

"'S shore 'nough a kindred thing to what raided that little Richards kid," he advised himself. "Looks like it might be afixin' for something even worse." He brushed at his forelock. "If only Ma was here with her doctorin'!"

But Ma's doctoring craft was now forever buried up by the spring. That is, he stared hard-eyed into the fireplace, unless such things had taken enough root in his mind that he could work out somewhat of a likeness. Some of it was onion poultices, he was sure. And turpentine with goose grease. Hot steam was good for opening up breathing, it seemed like. Mayhaps she put a little turpentine in that, too. Pa always claimed turpentine was good for everything but a busted leg and a bald head, and wouldn't hurt either of them. Rance prodded his mind for half-remembered cures he had seen Ma's nimble fingers compound. A latent thought prompted him to get the doorstep rock out of her bed and lay it beside the fire. Keeping it hot for her feet was most aidful in breaking up a cold fever.

Half an hour later, after plowing his way to the snow-banked roothouse, he had the pot of sliced onions simmering gently over the fire. He reached for the bag of brown sugar hanging from the ridgepole. It stuck in his mind that Ma put some sugar in with the poultice onions. Anyhow, sugar was helpful in most ailments, and it couldn't hurt anything. The turpentine and goose grease mixture stood ready in the heated tin cup. He guessed the cast-iron teakettle would have to make do for a steamer. The paper wrap from his new pants, shaped into a funnel, the big end to go over her face, should carry a fair amount of the steam to where it was most needed. He dumped the slightly cooked onions into a couple of salt sacks which had been stored against need in the occasional chest.

Another quick trip to the bedroom found no improvement in his charge. If anything, the shallow, raspy breathing seemed worse. Her cheeks felt alarmingly hot under his fingers. Rance bent closer, trying to make out more details in the dim light. He shook his head. A body couldn't do any rightful doctoring without he could see how to go about it. He laid the hot poultices down on the bedside stool while he hurried back to the outer room. A right smart thing it was, the way that storm had made him fill the candle box! He bent over the fireplace, lighting one in each hand. Set atop the chest of drawers, at the head of the bed, their glow sent his fear-laden spirits plunging to a new depth.

He hesitantly picked up one of the poultices, flattening it smoothly between his hands. He took a half step toward the bed. Sudden embarrassment, mixed with uncertainty, clutched at his feet. What would she think of a man fixing to do such a thing? He paused, half bent over, the breath sticking in his throat for a long moment. One hand moved to return the poultice to the stool. Yet this was a most needful thing. There was no other way! And Ma wouldn't look with much pridefulness on a body who let his shame-weakness be the death of a sick-taken stranger. He set the tin cup close beside him on the stool, then turned back toward the bed with all the shrinking qualms of a person facing a plunge into ice water.

"Miss—Miss Tenny!" He leaned tensely over the bed, stiff awkwardness fumbling his movements. "Miss Tenny, I-I gotta raise you up a mite to git this fixed. You don't pay me no mind; just do as I say."

She only moaned incoherently.

He stared at the ceiling, twisting at his forelock. Then, with sudden determination, he slid his hand blindly beneath her shoulders, lifting her body half erect. She only mumbled unintelligibly, with no sign of recognition. Might be she was too whipped out to be sensible of what was going on. The thought was encouraging. Further emboldened, he lifted her higher with one arm while undoing the upper buttons of nightgown and underwear so he could pull the garments away from her back. His free hand found the tin cup, quickly spreading a layer of the turpentined goose grease from her neckline to lower back. Then he snugged the poultice down against what he thought must be the lung cavity before pulling the underwear back in place. Expelling a long breath, he drew the nightgown tightly around her and laid her gently back down. He felt better already.

"Half done, Miss Tenny, slick as a whistle."

An eased mind and practiced hands found less trouble in greasing and poulticing her chest, so long as he kept his eyes averted from what no rightful intentioned male person had any business thinking about. It was bad enough to be making free with her body in such a way when she could only moan faintly as she stared at him with unseeing eyes. He quickly greased her throat and covered it with a piece of wool muffler.

Getting her to drink the hot whisky-sling was more difficult. It was lucky that Pa's emergency bottle was still half full, wasteful as she was in trying to swallow. A fair half of it was coughed back out, but he managed to get the rest down by coaxing her to sip a spoonful at a time.

He finally took the mug and spoon away. "I'll get that hot rock in next your feet in a minute, then fetch up the teakettle to give you a good steaming. Neither one won't be nothing to cause a pestering, though. You just lay back and rest easy." He hoped she understood some of what he was saying.

And after he had set the teakettle on the bedside stool with the funnel-like cone arranged to direct the steam against her face, he thought she was beginning to breathe easier. By evening chore time, he wasn't so sure. That hard rasping sound seemed to pick up force after he removed the teakettle. Her cheeks still held their feverish heat and the coughing had lost little of its hollow racking. Only the unintelligible mumbling and fretful head-tossing appeared to have quieted somewhat. He tucked the cover-quilt closer around her shoulders and carried the teakettle back to the fire for reheating.

"Might be that's enough to hold her till I git the stock tended," he reflected. "Then I'll have all evenin' to lay inta my doctorin'." He pulled at his forelock, slowly sinking to his knees. "Dear God," he concluded, "I'm free-givin' you all my thankfulness for lettin' Ma come back to help me out with her true knowin'. I couldn't nowise ahewed it out alone."

He rose to his feet and put more wood on the fire, then hung the teakettle back on the crane. It seemed he had more strengthening in his bones already. He shrugged into his coat and went outside. It was still snowing. He squinted up at the falling flakes. It looked like there was no pushing call to fret about what he should do with the girl. Between her sickness and the snowbound valley, he was plumb bogged down till the Lord gave him cause to do some later studying on it. Meanwhile, he had his hands nigh full of things that left scant room for outside thinking.

Old Brockle's soothing voice seemed to resolve any doubts about this decision. She munched her hay placidly in tune with the lazy chewing of the gray mare and the Buck mule. Rance finished his milking, settled in his conviction that things would right themselves, given the proper time.

Back at the cabin, he found little change. Tenny stirred restlessly at his touch when he visited the bedroom, but her mumbling voice still reflected the blankness in her eyes. He felt of the poultices. Both had lost most of their heat during his absence. He pulled the limp bags from beneath her nightgown and carried them outdoors. The half light of early dark obscured the soggy mass of cold onions he dumped out in the yard. It had started snowing harder, the rising wind rapidly drifting his path full. He hurried back into the cabin, dropping the door-bar firmly into its slots behind him.

It was almost a pleasure to slice up another pot of onions, while listening to the wind slat snow against the door. A rightly built house was a prideful thing to have this kind of weather. It made a body feel plumb rich to be gifted with so much of the Lord's favors. It was really a thing to ponder on, he thought, as he put the fresh onions over the fire. He let them simmer while he mixed another tin cup of grease. The bed-warming rock also needed reheating. He barely had time to strain the milk before the onions were ready to go into the odorous salt bags.

"This, with another good steamin', should give her ease till midnight," he reasoned hopefully. "Then a kindred one for the late night stretch. Agin I git her past the death-watch time, the worst oughta be dwindlin'."

Working the fresh poultices into position was a much smoother operation this time. He guessed it was her unknowing of how his hands touched her feverish body that lent him confidence in the task. The rewarmed rock was snugged back into the foot of the bed before he fed her the rest of the hot whisky-sling. It pleased him to see her sip the drink without fighting it, as she had before. And the teakettle steam seemed to have a more soothing effect, almost from the start. Rance hoped his wishful thinking hadn't built up a passel of misjudgment.

CHAPTER 7

It was a sputtering firebrand falling in on itself that stirred Rance into wakefulness one morning a week later. His head lifted groggily from forearms crossed on the split-log table, as the light probed through his tangled forelock. He hunched his shoulders against the shiver that ran up his spine. The fire was nearly out.

He felt like a sawdust man as he slid off the bench and stumbled across to the fireplace. One hand rubbed the gritty dryness out of his eyes while the other fumbled kindling sticks onto the bed of still live coals. The past days and nights blended into a hazy mixture of unreality. Nights were the worst; he hadn't dared surrender to the luxury of unblemished sleep. The poultices had to be renewed at regular intervals, new turpentined goose grease applied each time, the heavy teakettle kept steaming, and the bed-warming rock reheated with equal punctuality. He could only allow himself cat naps beside her bed, arousing every little while to determine the length of unburned candle, his only way of marking the passage of time. The days had been almost as demanding. There was wood to be carried for the insatiable fireplace, hurried trips to care for the stock, more onions to be sliced for fresh poultices, more food to be prepared (which he had little taste for and she was usually unable to eat). And, above everything else, there was always that hourly need to hurry back to her bedroom to make sure she hadn't uncovered herself or was in danger of choking on the phlegm which rose continually in her throat.

"I reckon," he assured himself, "that I needn't be fearful of the Devil gittin' a-holt of me, liken Pa's Bible book claims kin happen to them as idles time away."

One thing, his steady round of activities gave little room for the worry and uncertainty which added their silent weight to the more visible burdens. At times, the girl seemed to rally, lying limp and semi-conscious against her pillow. Then she would suddenly revert to the strangled breathing and feverish babblings that sent him to his knees in fervent prayers for both God's and Ma's help. It all left him struggling between hopeful relief and black despair. That one time, when she had looked up, wide eyes staring at him from the white pinched face, she seemed fully rational. There was normal comprehension in the look she gave him, when he answered her halting questions about where she was and who he was. Wild hope rose before him to flaunt its banner of victory won. Then, half an hour later, the specter of dismay crushed his chin back down on his chest, while he dejectedly wiped the bubbles of fresh phlegm from her lips to the old nightmare of unintelligible moaning. Rance felt his throat contract with a sense of bafflement that was almost a physical pain.

Day by day, she seemed to grow thinner and weaker. His efforts to feed her portions of the hot venison stew met only intermittent success. Mostly, it was a complete failure. Only on sporadic occasions would she swallow a few spoonfuls, when her labored breathing would ease momentarily.

Lack of a mirror saved Rance from discovering his own drawn face. Now he turned from the fire to shamble into the bedroom. His tired eyes tried to estimate the length of unburned candle on the chest of drawers. He knew he had overslept. His only hope was that it hadn't caused any damage. One knee braced itself against the bedstead as he reached beneath the quilt cover to search out the soggy poultices.

For a moment he stood transfixed, the poultice bag suspended from his hand. He sucked in his breath, his eyes flaring wide in wonderment. He slowly straightened his body, shaking his head to make sure he was awake. Then, with mouth still half-open on unvoiced questions, he again plunged his hand beneath the quilt. Yes, it was true; the flesh under his fingers was wet with sweat. He dropped his other hand onto the thin face. It, too, was moistly cool. He bent closer, making sure that his ears had not misinterpreted the soft and even breathing. But there was no mistake. The fever had definitely left her.

"Oh, God," he whispered, "you did save her!" The poultice dropped unheeded to the floor. "You done made the miracle happen! I'll be bearin' my thanks to you from here on out."

He sank weakly down on the stool and buried his face in his hands. Liken Pa always held, a body tries hard enough, the Lord has a way of rewarding his doings.

It was half an hour later that a faint stirring from the bed brought Rance in from the other room. He carefully balanced one of the maple-wood bowls in his hand. He felt like a new man. His eyes lighted sharply at sight of the wasted face looking up at him. It needed no second glance to tell him that the girl had her feet well clear of St. Peter's closing door.

"Heard you stir an' thought you might be famishin' for some vittles." He waved the bowl at her. "I've just been hottenin' up the stew an' made some fresh coffee. Figgered you might welcome it."

Her wan smile told him the big struggle was over. "I think I would like some of that." Her voice was little above a whisper, but it rang in his ears like an echo of the Liberty Bell. "It smells delicious."

"Fine! I was hopin' it would. But you stay covered up. I'll feed it to you." He eased the bowl down onto the stool while he settled himself on the edge of the bed. One hand reached for the sugar-sack handkerchief to tuck under her chin. His eye caught a movement beneath the quilt, and he shoved her arm back down.

"None of that!" he ordered. "You keep ever'thing under cover. That fever left you wet as a drowned rat an' weak as a frayed rope. Gotta git you dried out an' inta some other clo'es afore you dare face open air. Meanwhile, I'll spoon you some portions of this. Ma's doctorin' held to scanty feedin's by short spells after a fever. We'd best do that way now. She allus had the right of it."

Her weakness joined with his feeding judgment to halt the process before the bowl was half empty. She sank back limply, nodding her head over the last spoonful. Rance set the bowl on the stool while he straightened the pillow more comfortably and tucked the covers up over her shoulders. One hand lingered a moment on her cheek, noting no return of the feverish burning.

"You might try nappin' a mite now, whilst I red up the cabin. I've kinda let the inside work languish for want of time these last few days. Then, 'fore time for your next feedin', I'll rustle up some things for makin' you a change. It's needful that you be dried out an' bedded down proper-like 'fore night."

He tried to keep the exultation out of his voice as he picked up the bowl and discarded poultices. The latter he tossed into the fire with a grunt of relief. He wondered if he could ever stand the smell of onions again. However, his delight was too great to leave room for worrying about how he might feel later, about anything. He reached for the brush broom, as first aid to improvement of the littered floor.

His own bedding, he later decided, would have to do as a replacement for the wet quilts she lay in. He could take the latter for his own use, after drying them out. And Ma's other flannel nightgown would be all right for her to change into. Altogether, he guessed it would be easy enough to fix her up in fair shape for the night.

That is, it would be if he could figure out just how to do it. As weak as she was, most of it would be up to him. And changing both clothing and bedclothes for a helpless girl suddenly assumed outsize proportions. He pulled at his forelock, calling up all the gods of wisdom and sage advice.

Fortunately, the task proved to be less troublesome than he had expected. To change the bedding, it was only necessary to roll the girl enough to one side that he could lift the wet quilt and replace it with the dry one. A reverse turn enabled him to pull the soggy member entirely free and smooth down the other. Similarly, it was easy to drop the flannel nightgown down over her head, gingerly pulling free the wet one under its cover. She managed to work the new gown fairly well down into place by herself, doing whatever was necessary beneath it. Nevertheless, both were breathing unduly hard from their efforts by the time the exchange was made and he had tucked her into the cocoonlike nest of warm bedding. Rance felt his knees sag weakly as he went back for another bowl of broth.

Pa's open Bible book stared up at him from the far end of the table as he took down a clean bowl from the shelf cupboard. One glance set him to rubbing his eyes in an effort to stop the printed words from jumping all over the page. He guessed sleepiness was about to get its hooks into him. Mayhaps he could read something fitting to his thankfulness a little later, soon as this funny lightness went out of his head. He ladled up a bowlful of the broth and made his way unsteadily back to the bedroom.

The girl had relaxed into sort of a dull inertia. Rance felt his heart sink at first glance. He hurriedly set the bowl down on the stool. She soon roused under his touch, however. And her thin cheeks held the same moist coolness. He let his breath go in a long sigh of relief. Watching her come fully awake, under his move to prop her up on the pillow, was most heartening. That bit of exertion in changing to dry things hadn't hurt her, after all. When she almost emptied the second bowl of broth, without wasting scarcely a drop, only overpowering sleepiness prevented him from laughing with pure joy.

He remembered how her shoulders seemed to have doubled in weight when he laid her back down; but he never noticed the bowl falling from his nerveless hand as his long body slid into a boneless heap beside the bed. Her steady breathing was a rhythmic benediction, washing him into a bottomless sea of sleep.

Rance never knew how long he slept. Full daylight was filtering through the rawhide window when some subconscious call of duty nudged him awake. Cold and cramped, he sat up and rubbed his eyes. One hand strayed to his forelock. He hoped it was only morning of the first day. There was no call for a body to knuckle under, when it was needful to be on the job. He clawed himself upright, protesting muscles arguing with his thoughts about the rights of negligence.

But he guessed the girl had taken no hurt from it. She stirred drowsily as he leaned over the bed. Her lips curved in a weak smile as the brown eyes opened to focus on his face.

Her breathing carried none of the rasping harshness that had wracked her body for so long. He felt the wings of thankfulness waft him out into the other room.

Crouched over the fire, watching steam arise from the warming broth, he heard himself voice the belief that "Ma, or somebody, has shore been steerin' me along the right trail. It seems I done things with my hands that my mind reckoned naught of. It'd be right smart spooky, had anybody but Ma been hand-leadin' me through such a ruckus."

This same sense of spiritual guidance was intensified when he went in to find a greatly revived girl wondering if she couldn't have some meat and other solids added to her next feeding of broth. Rance was delighted. Hunger was a big step on the road to recovery. He lost no time in chopping up a generous portion of meat and the last of the vegetables to thicken the broth. Second thought also suggested he scour out the mush pot for a mess of that old shanty wife pudding Ma used to make of rice, raisins, and dried apples. He put the dried apples to soak immediately, while "Oh! Susanna" rose unbidden to his lips.

The rightness of things followed him outdoors. It had stopped snowing. A late forenoon sun had stolen through a rift in the clouds to turn the world into a spotless realm of dazzling brightness. The whole clearing sparkled as though strewn with new-cut diamonds, each glittering gem a gift designed for his special pleasure. Rance felt his heart swell with a great sense of fulfillment, aided by Ma's craft. Even the old woodpecker seemed to be drumming his approval of it all. He thought he had never seen such a wonderful day. "Oh! Susanna" took on something symbolic of a paean of praise as he floundered his way out to do the barn chores.

Later, back at the cabin, he found the girl clear-eyed and a strong touch of color in her cheeks.

"Oh, Tenny!" he blurted through tight lips, "yo're far on the road to bein' all right." Something unexplainable surged through his body to set his limbs trembling and his voice sound like a mouth harp with half the keys missing. "All you need now is plenty of stoutenin' grub. And I'll feed you that as fast as I dare."

The ghost of a smile lighted her pinched face in reply. He brushed the black hair back from her brow, noticing the healthy warmth of cheeks and neck. How pitifully thin she was; she must have lost twenty pounds! It would take a plumb heap of feeding to fetch her back to prime. Still, that shouldn't be too hefty a job, now that the real danger was past.

"Why do you call me Tenny?" she asked out of a long silence. "Didn't I tell you my name is Felicity–Felicity Gatewood?"

Rance fingered his straw-colored forelock. Had she actually mentioned her name? He couldn't remember any such thing.

"I musta been asleep, if you bespoke it," he said at last. "But I did rec'lect you saying you was from Tennessee. That's where I got the Tenny. It seemed to fit you nigh on perfect, so I've been thinkin' thataway. I hope you won't take it unkindly. I reckon as how I kin learn to say Fell–Flis–Flicity."

"Never mind." Her smile was almost a laugh. "I believe I like Tenny much better. 'Tenny!'" She ran the word over under her breath. "That name sounds nice. I don't think I ever really cared for Felicity. It's—it's—oh, it always seemed to be so much of a mouthful."

Rance grinned his relief. It was sure kindly of her to take his gift name, without all the backing and filling most women would have done.

"Then we'll let it go as Tenny?"

"If you like. That suits me."

"Good! But I'll just let you study on it for faults, whilst I go round up some more vegetables. Can't run shy of stuff needful for buildin' you up—Tenny."

He rolled the word "Tenny" over in his thoughts as he made his way out to the roothouse. The wooden shovel, dragging along behind him, seemed to be whispering the name in a tuneful way as it slid over the snow. It was sure a right pretty name. And it sounded better all the time, especially when he picked up the refrain with his voice. It went uncommonly well with Gatewood, too, he decided.

It was right down too bad, now, that she didn't have a face pretty enough to match the name. That overwide mouth, eyes as big as coat buttons, and cheeks sunk in like old Grandma Hardig's, just before she died, made her somewhat unsightly to look at. But mayhaps some fattening up would ease the worst of that. He hoped so. Anyhow, the makeup of a body's face was no killing matter. She looked to be a right nice girl otherwise. However, it was naught for him to fret about, not on such a purely handsome day as this.

Even the heavy snowdrift piled against the roothouse door failed to disturb his lighter mood. He shoveled it clear, almost without thinking. And when he shoved open the grass-insulated door, his spirits rose even higher. Despite the days of bitter cold and wind-driven snow, the insde showed no sign of frost. In fact, the place was nearly as warm as the leanto bedroom. It seemed, as he inspected his handiwork before filling the firkin with assorted vegetables, that Pa spoke a right smart bit of truth, when he claimed that after-dark miserables never tromped down on a man who done his work rightly proper in the daytime.

CHAPTER 8

The following days passed swiftly. Tenny was up in the cherrywood rocker by the end of the week. She complained that he was making an invalid of her by not letting her help with the work; but he contended there was no logic in shutting the door and then leaving the window open. As weak as the sickness had left her, she'd hold off exerting herself till she had enough stoutness built up to carry her along, or he would tie her to the bed. He wasn't about to let any such nonny ideas trap him into another set-to with lung fever, or whatever it was. And that was that! She was forced to accept his decision, secretly glad in her own heart that nothing active was expected of her.

Seated in the cherrywood rocker, drawn close to the fire and with a warm cover-quilt tucked closely about her, she found herself often relieved to hear him announce that her up-and-about period was finished for that day. Despite the resented feeling of uselessness, it was a welcome relief to surrender herself to the comfortable bed and the five feedings a day that he demanded.

"I never saw anybody so stubborn," she told him one afternoon. "You must sit up nights practicing it."

"Well, I'm not aimin' to let you cozen me inta no foolishment at this stage of the game," he countered. "You're due to make out right sprightly, long as we go easy by jerks. But there's no sense in lettin' speed run the wheels off the wagon midway of the journey. Anyhow, there's only a triflin' to do, 'sides takin' things easy-like whilst we're snowbound."

"All right, stubborn!" She stuck out her tongue at him. "You have the whip hand now. But just you wait—"

"Threatenin', eh?" He helped her back to the bedroom, a mocking grin on his face. "Well, we'll build that bridge when we find a crick to cross. Meanwhile I claim the rights of salvage."

As the days passed, however, both saw that she was steadily gaining strength under his ministrations. It was a morning for mutual rejoicing when he came in from milking to find her dishing up the cornmeal mush before the fireplace. Though he insisted on her staying indoors another week, the resilience of youth eventually asserted itself in proclaiming the passing of danger. It was not until then that he allowed her to bundle up in the warmest things they could find for occasional walks about the yard.

The ensuing weeks brought a growing sense of well-being to both of them. Returning health found Tenny ever more eager to be of help. Gone, she said, were the old days of drying dishes or preparing vegetables while swaddled up in the cherrywood rocker. Rance was forced to lay aside his anxious protestations as he watched her go on to more active things without harming herself. Almost before either of them fully realized it, their lives had settled into an unplanned division of labor.

It was a comfortable feeling, needing no words of explanation. Tenny accepted her position as might a shipwrecked sailor washed ashore on some verdant isle. Yesterday was dead; tomorrow a blank. She could only accept today's blessings of life and security with a deep sense of obligation which time might help her to repay.

Rance, on the other hand, had no particular feeling one

way or another. Rescuing Tenny and helping her through her illness had been only the common decency expected of any normal person faced by another's misfortune. Such things occasionally happened to nearly everybody. He guessed he had been just plain lucky in being able to handle it. He could think of himself as little more than sort of a choreboy, working under the direction of God, Fate, and what he could remember of Ma's doctoring. As such, he was purely glad the job was finished, with everything coming out as well as it had. Anyhow, she was now more than evening things up by the way she kept the cabin always neat, besides taking over the cooking. It was a caution the way she could brighten everything up, just by keeping the place to rights and leaving him to the necessary outside work, without him having to fret about the fire or what to get for the next meal.

Altogether, it seemed that everything had worked out in a truly prideful way. Without her troubles bringing them together, he would have had a pretty dismal time of it, penned up in the cabin by this big snowfall, with naught to do except wallow in his empty lonesomeness. By similar figuring, she, lacking his luck in finding her and pulling her through the bad sickness, would probably have died a couple of times without anybody ever knowing it. Yes, sir, it rightly looked as how they'd both been favored uncommonly well by whoever was casting watchful eyes on this corner of the country.

Mayhaps this big snowfall was even a part of it, holding him off from a heap of worry about her next move. Like as not that part would all come clear in his mind as soon as a warm spell unblocked the trails for travel. Meanwhile, he might as well shuck off unthrifty ponderings while enjoying the scad of bounties that had been showered down, liken the "Providings" Pa always held was a thing God would set his hand to in due time, should the need be of the deserving kind.

Rance found that the decision to close his mind against what could be neither helped nor immediately anticipated had twofold results. Freed from useless speculation on whatever solution time might see fit to present at some unknown date, his thoughts were more at liberty to expand under the warmth of a cheerful home and good company. This spontaneous pleasure in everything about him was reflected by Tenny's happiness in apparently having all she wanted to make her life enjoyable. On such a frictionless meeting ground, they quickly drifted into the comfortable routine of homelike ease.

Evenings were the best. Then, with the chores out of the way, supper over, the cabin tidied up, candles alight, and fire blazing merrily, they felt themselves far apart from the throes of a world given over to warring elements. Tenny's great delight was to cuddle down in a patchwork quilt, sunk deep in the cherrywood rocker, while the wind in the chimney howled its harmless threats at the blazing logs and snow beat its wild tattoo against the roof. Her smile of unblemished contentment would be as warming to Rance as the fire that lighted the blanket on which he sprawled beside the hearth. At such times, they would often spend uncounted hours poring over Pa's Bible book or the dog-eared almanac. Rance discovered an unknown delight in the way she would pronounce the hard words and read whole pages without stumbling over the sentences. At times, she did even better than Pa in making the reading really meaningful.

"You musta had a heap of book learnin' back in Tennessee," he said one night, as she finished a chapter and laid the Bible book aside. "You make the words slide along like water out of a spring. I dunno as I ever heard the beat of it."

"Oh, it's easy, once you get started right." She laughed down at his flushed face, cuddled on one arm in the firelight. "Or maybe I just had a gift for it. My teachers always spoke well of my reading. And Mother taught me quite a lot, after I had to quit school in the sixth grade to help at home. She put a great store in education, especially good reading; reading, she always insisted, is the foundation of knowledge. And it is something anybody should be able to do, by practice and some attention to spelling."

"I see! Mayhaps that's the secret. I never worked at it enough to rightly git the hang of it. We somehow never lived around where there were much of any schools. 'Sides, I was usually tol'able busy with other things. Pa kinda steered me to a fair understandin' of the simpler kind, when he had time; but Ma an' me, we mostly left it to him for the reg'lar readin'." He sat up and folded his arms thoughtfully around his knees. One hand fingered the bristly forelock. He spoke hesitantly: "Might be you could sorta herd me in the right direction for catchin' the how of it, if you was so minded. I reckon it's something a body should know the true handlin' of."

"Why, I'd be glad to! It's mostly a matter of familiarizing yourself with the words until they form sort of a pattern. And now is a splendid time to start."

She handed him the big Bible, then slid down on the fireplace hearth beside him.

Rance heaved himself over on one elbow, propping the book up to catch the light to best advantage. His mouth screwed up to shape the words, he read haltingly, one forefinger tracing the lines. But try as he would, he could not make anything sound the way Tenny had spoken it.

He looked up with a scowl. "I misdoubt I kin ever hew a true line in this kind of timber. There's too many gnarly knots for my brand of an axe."

"Oh, it will come easier with a little practice. Reading is like any other kind of new work for you. As stubborn as you are, you'll get the best of it in a short while. Learning the knack of proper pronunciation and sounding out the syllables of longer words will clarify everything. That won't take long. Here, let me show you!"

Rance said, a week later, that he knew how a green colt felt when it was first hitched to a wagon. If he hadn't been tied down to seemingly endless evenings in the snowbound cabin, he'd surely have kicked loose and taken to the hills.

"But," Tenny countered gaily, "you have now steadied down and learned to pull the load. I am really proud of the way you are progressing. You will be a first-class reader in no time."

"If you an' the snow hold out long enough." He grinned self-consciously. "But now that I've whipped old Hezekiah an' Ephraim, it looks like I might stand to weather the rest of it. It's a mark to keep my sights on."

And his sighting did improve. Each day found his studies coming easier. Less and less did Tenny have to point out the proper division of compound words or intricacies of pronunciations. More and more did he succumb to the fascination of the printed lines, the prideful ability of being able to conquer whole sentences without floundering over meaningless combinations of letters. And with this arrived the intriguing discovery of the hidden delights to be found in the next paragraph. It was a voyage into a strange new land. He, the explorer, reveled joyously in each fresh scene, only to plunge avidly on to the next. Evening after evening, he pursued this exciting quest under Tenny's supervision, until his voice rasped hoarsely and gritty weights dragged down his eyelids.

Later, as his skill increased, they would take turns reading aloud throughout the evening. Such reading periods would be gauged by a stick laid across the bed of coals: when the stick burned in two, it marked the time for the other's turn. Then another stick of uniform size would be set afire to denote the next exchange. They had worked their way well into the Bible book, digested the almanac, and were struggling with Pa's battered copy of *David Copperfield* as the days ran up into December.

CHAPTER 9

Rance said, "It 'pears liken we had us a right lofty richness in all these nicety things aclamorin' for our notice."

"I agree!" Tenny nodded over the wooden dish trough. "Blessed with so much good comfort and security, along with more pleasure and entertainment than we ever have time for, I don't see how anyone could feel richer."

Rance pulled at his forelock, contentment mirroring his face. He couldn't think of anything more that was worth the bother of fretting over. Of course, some things were a mite faulty, in one way or another. The outside work, now, was quite a chore. The feeding and milking pulled a body out in the cold as regular as daylight and dark. Chopping a hole in the creek ice and then hazing the animals out of the warm barn to sink their muzzles in the frigid stream was just as regular, and even colder. Still, looking at it in the right spirit, such things gave a body some good exercise to shake off the stagnation of steady house living. And what frosty edges the stock tending left could always be worked off in cutting wood for the ravenous fireplace. The daily trips out to the springhouse and roothouse for water and vegetables didn't really amount to a great sight, being mostly a freshener after a spell in the cabin. Altogether, it averaged out mighty favorable to a body setting himself up to be a going concern. And he wasn't addle-witted enough to figure on picking roses without running against a few thorns, as Pa always said.

And then there was Tenny. Fortune truly favored a body who had such as her to keep the cabin in shape and fix up all kinds of tasty vittles, whilst he was doing needful things outside. Looking back on it, he failed to see how he had made out as well as he did by himself before she came along. Nor was that all. Now that she was fattening up to prime condition and bubbly good nature, just having her about the house was a thing to cipher out the few rough spots in the trail—which, come to think on it, didn't rightly amount to much in the long run.

This last, he felt, was especially true when they settled down for a long evening together. Reading aloud to each other had never lost its charm. Their second journey through the world of *David Copperfield* was much smoother and, to Rance, far more meaningful. Then there were long games of Odd and Even, played with a handful of beans, or that old favorite, Parcheesi, using a charcoal-marked sandstone slab for a board. When Rance uncovered Ma's old kaleidoscope hidden down among other oddities in one corner of the occasional chest, they found a most welcome pastime in patiently watching the shifting patterns of color it would display. He guessed he would never forget how Tenny laughed till she cried at his story of Ma's efforts to correct his childhood way of calling the instrument a "kapeedilcope." Often they would thus lay aside books and games in favor of lighthearted banter or serious exchange of ideas. To both, this seemed to be generous recompense for whatever unwelcome difficulties happened to fall in their way.

"How about putting a little life into that fire?" Tenny turned from stacking the two china plates, two heavy mugs, and the tin pie plate back on the shelf cupboard. "Another minute and you'll be sound asleep in a stone-cold house."

"Hunh? Oh, all right!" Rance roused from his abstraction,

hunching himself forward on hands and knees. "I reckon's how I just sorta got myself led astray by a bunch of thinkin'."

He rolled some fresh log-chunks onto the fire, then turned back to the pair of slim willows he had been fashioning into snowshoe frames. His plan for putting out a string of traps demanded some way of keeping himself up on top of the yard-deep snow. He didn't know anything about making snowshoes, aside from what he had seen of that pair hanging in the trader's store at Oregon City. Yet lacing a web into a simple frame didn't seem like such a tough job. He wished he had some heavy rawhide for the webbing; logic suggested it as the proper material. He guessed, however, he would have to make out with strings of twisted cedar bark. As tough as the bark was, it should be tolerable lasting. Anyhow, it was the only thing in sight.

"Even having to restring 'em a time or two wouldn't be too bad," he reasoned. "Providin' I make out to git enough furs for a summer grubstake."

"You will!" Tenny sat down beside him to resume twisting the long strands of bark into thin cords. "That big pond up the creek must be full of beaver, and there are ever so many other animals all through the woods. I see nothing for you to worry about, if these snowshoes keep you from burying yourself in the snow."

Her firm assurance proved to be right. Crude and awkward though they were, the new snowshoes were a great help in getting about over the snow-banked country. Later, experience combined with a gradually hardening trail to make travel easy and comparatively swift. Rance found a singular pleasure in being able to walk wherever the urge directed, unmindful of the depth of snow; it gave him a vague sense of mastery over the elements which, though lurking deep in his subconscious, was none the less most exhilarating.

The only sour note was the rapierlike end of a broken limb which sheared through the bark cords one afternoon when he stepped off the trail to look at a marten trap. The rest of his way home was made at kind of a limping, lopsided gait, trying to keep his weight on the one good snowshoe, but his discomfort was largely offset by the splendid otter pelt which crowned his day's take of furs. Nor was the repair of the damaged webbing anything to cry about, he decided, replacing the severed cords after a generous supper of Tenny's delicious beaver-tail soup. As a matter of fact, the extra evening's work of reconditioning the snowshoe was more or less lost sight of in the fun of describing his day's adventures and gloating over the fine otter pelt.

"It's really surprising the amount of choice furs you have taken this winter," she remarked, joining him in fleshing and stretching the skins. "You must have dollars and dollars' worth already."

"Done pretty well," he admitted with a satisfied grin. "I have to fetch in a scad of extras to cover the share you're earnin' in helpin' me flesh an' stretch every night."

"You don't owe me anything for that. I am glad to help what I can. Besides, think of all the muskrat and beaver meat you bring home, not to mention the grouse, quail, squirrels, and rabbits. The way you provide such a variety of food, along with the comforts and security you've given me, is something I can never repay, no matter how much work I do. Then there is that pine squirrel you brought me for a pet. I never will be able to show my appreciation for that."

"Oh, that was nothin' much." He glanced up at the squirrel, busily opening prune pits on the mantel. "The little feller's busted leg had him headed for a starvin' death. All I did was fetch him along. You did the real work, carin' for him and the feedin' an' all, till he got back his strength."

"Stubborn as ever about claiming any credit!" Her laugh sent the squirrel scampering up to the top of the shelf cupboard. "I suppose you would even foist your good fur harvest off on something besides yourself, if you could think of a way."

"Luck!" He grinned back at her. "Luck an' makin' steady rounds every day."

It was nice to be appreciated, even though he didn't deserve it. The thought was running through his mind with pleasurable warmth a couple of days later. He was on his way home, musing over the good things of life, when the sight of two barren does under a brushy, low-hanging fir brought him sharply to attention. He dropped silently behind a stump and brought up the heavy rifle. It was an easy shot. The other deer only stared around inquiringly at the muffled sound of the gunshot half buried in the snow. It fell almost on top of the other. A wide grin split Rance's face as he surveyed this answer to their basic meat needs for the rest of the winter.

Tenny came out to help dress the animals when he dragged them up to the cabin behind the gray mare. She was surprisingly handy with a knife, Rance remarked, straightening up to watch her movements.

"I guess I shouldn't be too awkward at it." Her lips curved in the smile that made little wrinkles run up the sides of her nose. "Not after all the hogs I helped Father butcher, growing up on our Tennessee farm. He was a good teacher."

"Your folks musta been real big-timey farmers?" He spoke questioningly. "All them butcher hogs an' ever'thing?"

"Razorbacks!" Memory sharpened her voice to a thin edge. "Razorback hogs and scarecrow cows that ran in the brush and fed on acorns. We poor white hill-farmers couldn't be choosy. That's why I had to quite school in the sixth grade. That's why Mother was always ailing with something we had no way of curing. That's why Father decided to come West, where it was said good health favored everybody and free land would produce everything from six-foot corn to pokes of gold nuggets. That's why—"

She broke off sharply, ducking her head to hide the sudden quiver of her lips.

Rance made a big show of rolling the deer over to free the skin along its backbone. His ears still echoed the quick intake of her breath, followed by abrupt silence. He reckoned he knew about how she felt.

"Might nigh the same as we'uns over in Missouri," he said lightly, to break the tension. "Pa figgered we'd lived on hogs, grits, an' hominy long enough, so we lit out for the land of milk an' honey. He held that quality folks was only the harvest of ambition an' opportunity. Seein's he had a scad of ambition, he set out to gamble a long ride on the Oregon country's opportunities h'istin' us up inta the boiled-shirt class."

"Hm-m-m!" She studied a broken fingernail for a moment. "What made your father think that opportunity was so much better away back here in the hills than down among the other settlers?"

"Well-l, Pa didn't much cotton to close neighbors. He allus held that crowdin' too many apples in a barrel was sure to start rot asettin' in. When he went scoutin' for a donation claim, he kept shy of the main valley. He sighted all that flat land as settlin' up liken a growth of sunflowers, all bent on smotherin' each other to dyin' for want of standin' room. He claimed findin' this spot was like findin' Ma; there was naught better to look for. That big, open meadow stretchin' clean up past the big beaver dam, the good pasture, flowin' crick, an' plenty of needful timber was all the future he wanted. And to make it just right, there was this circle of hills h'isted up all around, liken their weddin' ring, to keep him an' Ma safe from them as would pester their holdings."

"I think I see his point. And it was your stubborn nature that held you to his plans, despite obstacles."

"Well, it woulda been a shirkin' thing to sneak off, liken a whipped pup. Neither Pa nor Ma would think kindly of a body doin' that."

"No, I suppose not." She paused a moment, her eyes studying the sky. "Not with you being all that's left of their big dream," she finished.

"It looks somewhat liken I was left on purpose to make their dreams pan out." Rance turned to face the girl, his eyes lifting over her head to circle the big meadow. "Pa allus claimed that if the seed was any good, the crop was bound to keep improvin'. I'd feel mighty piddlin'-like was I to backset what he started."

Tenny nodded slowly, wiping her bloody knife clean on the snow. Her face was grave with thought.

"That's something for me to remember, when I get to feeling sorry for myself," she said at last. "I hope I can keep that in mind till I can see myself doing the things Mother always hoped for herself."

"You will! We will! It's mostly holdin' our sights on the mark we set up. I reckon it's sort of like a job our folks laid out for us to handle whilst they were off someplace. We can't nowise let 'em down."

"Well, we'll do a lot of trying, if that's the way it is." The quick smile crinkled her nose up at him as she turned to go back into the cabin. "And the first big try might be for you to let me cut your hair. You look like an unsheared billygoat."

Rance grinned at her back as she walked toward the cabin. There was no use trying to argue with Tenny. She'd stir an idea till the pot boiled over. Anyhow, he guessed a haircut wouldn't hurt anything, aside from letting the cold chaw at his neck. And he might as well knuckle under and get it over with, before she thought up any more likenesses to shiftless hill-folks or billygoats or something worse.

Watching her walk across the yard, he noticed for the first time how patched and thin her dress had become. And there was no denying the bedraggled skirt bottom, stained and faded from its ordeal in the snow during the Indian attack and too many washings in the following weeks. She was downright needful of some new clothes! If town wasn't so far away, and the snow so deep! He kicked at the deer hide and shook his head. Some things sure outvoted a body.

The thought, however, was not to be shunted off. A germinating idea slowly brightened his eyes. Buckskin, now, made a right nice dress. Many hard-put pioneer women wore them, traded from the Indians. They looked plumb handsome, too, a lot of them. And if the dumb Indians could fashion them, it shouldn't be much of a chore for any half-bright white man to do the same.

He studied the two deer hides at his feet. With the one from earlier in the fall, these should make enough material to fit her out. He figured he could make out with the tanning all right, recalling the things Pa had told him about the Indians' way. It seemed middling easy, and he had plenty of time while the snow had him shut up. Yes, sir, he'd bet Tenny would look as handsome as a sparkly Christmas tree, once she was rigged out in white buckskin, mayhaps trimmed up some with the beads he had scratched out of that old Indian campground last summer. A Christmas tree! His thoughts jumped as though struck head-on by Tenny's imaginary billygoat. The very thing! Just the kind of a surprise fixing he had been prodding his mind for to make her Christmas extra special. He felt like he had suddenly swallowed a balloon.

CHAPTER 10

Back at the cabin, however, the balloon quickly began to shrink under the weight of thought. Working the hides soft would have to be done mostly in the cabin, where it was warm. That would be an open invitation for anybody as peart as Tenny to suspect something. Worse yet, what did he know about cutting and fitting a dress? Hunh-uh! The whole idea of a surprise was a right down witless notion. He pulled at his forelock. It looked like about the only way would be for him to tell her the whole thing, then have her help with it. Mayhaps that would work out just as well as a surprise, in the long run. Anyhow, she might have surprise enough to do her, when she got that cedar chest he was building out in the barn at odd times.

It was a busy period for Rance Hardig. The days he had been marking off in the almanac seemed to be overtaking Christmas with astonishing speed. Along with his regular work, there was the cedar chest he was trying to finish. Starting with rough boards, split out of a length of butt cedar, he had to scrape each piece smooth with his knife and Pa's old block plane. Then came the tedious job of polishing them with fine sand under a wooden block, before fastening them together with whittled oak pegs. Sometimes he almost despaired of ever getting it completed. Only the thought of Tenny's first Christmas away from her folks kept him at it.

Now the prospective buckskin dress arose to claim more of his time. The deer hides had to be cleaned of all meat and fat, then soaked in wood ashes until the hair loosened enough to be scraped off. More scraping and working was then needed to remove the tough membranous inner surface and residue of the ash-water soaking. Much time was consumed in stirring the hides about in the tanning solution of deer brains, lye soap, and water. Then came the big task of drying and working them between the hands and over a sharpened stake, to break up the grain and bring them to their ultimate soft pliability. Rance often worked until the small hours of the night in transforming a stubborn hide into the desired dry, raglike, finished buckskin.

"What are you going to use those hides for, when you get them tanned?" Tenny asked one evening, curiosity overcoming her idle interest.

"Oh—ah—" Rance squinted an eye at the pine squirrel perched on her shoulder, determination to hang onto his surprise as long as possible spurring his thoughts. "Figgered they'd come in handy for something," he finished lamely. "You got any suggestions?"

"They would make a nice cover for this rough log table."

"Now that's a thought, Tenny." He pulled at his forelock. "I've just been danglin' along, reasonin' that time'd scare up the most needful way to use 'em, sooner or later."

"Just like you've been dangling along about having your hair cut. If you don't let me tend to it sooner, you'll be using it to stuff a bedtick later."

"Now you shouldn't be frettin' over little things like that so much. Pa allus held that frettin' over things was bound to hinder the digestion, overstrain the heart, an' cause upsets of the liver." He grinned up at her, glad to have the subject changed. "But I'll lay off tomorra an' let you shear it. We'll git at it soon's I finish chorin', lest you forget to r'mind me."

Tenny wasn't one to forget. Nor was she wrong in her

opinion of his needs. Rance had never fully realized how long his hair had grown until he saw the pile of clippings around his feet and felt the nakedness of his neck.

"Shoulda held off till spring thaw," he said ruefully, rubbing the denuded neck as he backed up to the fireplace. "You'll need to wrap me up in a wool sock agin I go outside."

"Or turn the housework over to you? I could do the chores, rather than have the cold snap you off at the neck."

He tossed another stick onto the fire. "Oh, I'll survive, even if I have to make me a wig out of a horse tail. That'd beat washin' up all these cookin' things."

"You did pretty well at that before."

"Uh-huh! That was just make-do whilst I was shapin' you up inta something useful. Had to build me a housekeeper if I aimed to git caught up with outdoor things."

She wrinkled her nose and stuck out her tongue as she attacked the scattering of hair with the brush broom. It was fun to match wits with Rance; he was always ready for a joke, while never getting mad or sarcastic.

He had started most of this banter soon after she was up and around. It was his idea that a bit of foolishness would brighten her days and help soften the worst bitterness of her tragedy. It seemed to be good medicine. After the first few weeks, her despondent weeping, or dry-eyed grief, slowly vanished under blooming health and more general light-heartedness.

Her changed attitude was Rance's chief delight. Having her gay companionship was an ever-fresh wonder. No more did he have to work himself into drugged insensibility in order to find a sleep that was free of tortured misery; no more were his working days haunted by the double grave below the spring; no more was stark loneliness a grim specter staring over his shoulder. He need only think of Tenny to feel himself surrounded by comforting care and cheerful friendship, all the horrible emptiness of the past mercifully shunted aside. It was a strange and fascinating sensation, like emerging into some shining place of peace and beauty, after long confinement in the darkness of a dungeon. Everything was different since she came. The cabin had taken on new life and color; idle time was an exciting journey into new worlds; succeeding storms had turned the drabness of outdoors into a shining white wonderland.

As for Tenny herself, each day heightened her transformation from the bedraggled, hopeless waif to a creature aglow with life and vitality. She was even getting to be right sightly to look at, Rance told himself, now that her face was plumping out and her hair had got over its likeness to a yarn mop. The way it shone in the firelight, the black curls framing her wide brown eyes, made a right handsome picture, any way you looked at it. He wished he could think of more things that would birth those sudden smiles that seemed to spread clean up to her eyes, like a springtime dawn over a flowery hillside. All she needed, he decided, was some fitting clothes to replace that dingy old dress. White buckskin, now, made trim and dainty, should set her off like a picture-book lady. He felt his mind squirm in anticipation.

It was a heady secret. He had all he could do to hold onto his surprise as long as possible. Christmas was only a week away when the flight of time compelled him to tell her the purpose of the new buckskins. He wasn't sure how long it would take to make the dress, but half a dozen evenings should allow enough leeway, without the chance of overunning Christmas completely.

"How about switchin' over to Ma's old, patched-up dress for a couple hours?" he proposed, as they finished clearing up the supper things that evening. "We could use that one you've got on for a pattern."

"A pattern for what?" She stopped in her tracks, turning to face him.

"Well-l, I was sorta fixin' to rig you up a new dress for Christmas. Now, I'm kinda stuck for the knowin' how to handle the job. You bein' the only help I've got in that line, I'm purely havin' to bring your present out in the open afore times, so you kin show me how to tackle it." He reached the tanned hides down from the peg in the wall to spread them out on the table. "Seein's you've only got the one dress. I couldn't figger anything but usin' it for a pattern, along with you to do the cuttin' out an' makin' it fit."

"You mean—you mean you tanned the hides for me? You did all that work pretending they were for nothing special?" Her eyes were wide with dawning happiness as she impulsively reached up to kiss him on the cheek. "Oh, Rance, that's the nicest thing anybody ever did for me!"

Rance tugged at his forelock, squirming his embarrassment. He touched his cheek with one finger, to see if it was really afire. His mouth closed slowly.

"'Tain't nothin' but an idea, Tenny, something boundin' to heap another chore onta you, was you kindly disposed to do it. I'm plumb sorry I couldn't finish it unbeknownst to you, liken I planned, but it sorta got me treed. About the onliest thing left was to ruin your surprise an' dump the heft of the work onta you. It'll be mostly like me cozenin' you inta makin' yourself a Chris'mas present."

"Don't think that for a minute, Rance Hardig! Doing it together will make it all the more Christmasy. You are a dear to think of such a splendid thing!" She almost sang the words as she ran into the bedroom to change.

And her pleasure grew each evening, as they cut buckskin

to match the old gingham bodice, then decided to let the skirt fall slim and straight to her ankles. Using an awl and bone needle to saw the parts together with fine buckskin thongs was a slow and laborious process. Decorating the waist front with the old Indian beads was even slower. None of this, however, dimmed the joy of accomplishment. The sheer fun of working together, often joining their voices in the old Southern mountain melodies, was an added delight. Rance thought he had never known so much pure satisfaction and contentment.

A further pleasure was stealing time from his regular daytime work to finish the cedar chest. This was a definite surprise she would have no inkling of until Christmas morning. Secreted in the barn, under the guise of caring for the stock, he finished pinning it together with the pegs whittled from dry oak heartwood, and hinged the lid with pieces of cunningly contrived deer horn. The final sanding had left the wood smooth as velvet. Now he brought out the rich color and final glow by rubbing it full of the oil drained out of the deers' shank bones. He ran his finger lovingly over its surface as he hid it away under the barn eaves overhead.

It was two days before Christmas that he brought the graceful little fir tree home on his way from running the trap line. It was a special tree that he had located weeks before, standing alone up on the rocky hillside, where wind and weather had shaped it into a sturdy cone of unblemished symmetry. With the dress now completed, they spent the following afternoon in decorating the tree with bits of colored paper, found in the occasional chest, and tufts of undamaged cotton from the scraps of quilt that had wrapped Tenny's legs against the cold during her ride through the storm. Rance secured it upright in a firkin filled with rocks. Finished, they both stood back to proclaim their delight in the "prettiest thing west of

Fort Hall!" Evening found them shouting their joy as they danced around it, their voices blending in the old familiar Christmas carols.

Later, with the pet squirrel cuddled in his shirt front, Rance pretended to read an extra chapter in the Bible book while Tenny was in the bedroom making ready for bed. Not until all was quiet in the other room did he slip out to get the cedar chest. Then, concealing the gift under his mackinaw, he was so intent on positioning it to his satisfaction, without noise or disturbance, that he failed to notice the small bundles that had been tucked well back under the tree during his absence.

Thus it was that Christmas morning brought equal surprises to both of them. Rance had just brought the fireplace coals back to a dancing, cheerful blaze when Tenny walked into the room. She was trim and dainty in the new dress. The white buckskin, with its fringe along yoke, sleeves, and skirt seams lending fresh beauty to her youthful body curves, moved Rance to declare her plumb handsome as the Christmas tree. His admiring glance swept down from the jet-black curls and brown eyes, still softly moist from sleep, to follow the lines of snug-fitting bodice and loose, straight skirt. He pulled at his forelock, his wide grin slowly shaping itself to the notes of "Oh! Susanna." Never, he thought, had he seen anything so right down purely fetching.

"Prettier'n a young doe in a mountain meadow!" he murmured under his breath. "Or a patch of lupine aswayin' in the breeze, while daybreak crawls up behint the Siskiyou Peaks."

Tenny, however, seemed to have completely forgotten the new dress. Down on her knees, both arms wrapped lovingly around the cedar chest, she was almost tearful in her rapture.

She ran a hand gently over the satiny wood, looking up with moist eyes.

"You made this just for me!" she cried, springing suddenly to her feet and hugging him fiercely. "Oh, Rance, what a beautiful thing! I simply adore it! It's so wonderful! How can I ever thank you?"

"Don't try!" he answered, the warmth of satisfaction struggling with pretended indifference. "I'm just glad if it pleasures you. 'Tain't much, but was the best I could do, bein' snow-blocked ag'inst goin' anywheres for boughten things." He patted her shoulder awkwardly. "I wanted some sort of a nicety for your Christmas."

"Well, this is it! Nothing could be nicer, in town or anywhere."

"Just like you," he broke in, the words surprising even himself. "You look like the flower of the world in that new dress."

"Thanks to your tanning of the hides and helping me with most of the work on it. And speaking of clothes, it was nice of you to dress up for this special day."

He glanced down at his new store pants and shoes, one hand instinctively smoothing his shortened hair. He was glad he had taken time to shave before going to bed. Then he forgot everything else as she began pulling his gifts out from beneath the tree. He blankly stared his surprise as she uncovered the wool socks, two pairs of mittens, and the long muffler, all recently knitted from the yarn Ma had left in the cherrywood rocker. The bowl of homemade sugar candy was no less surprising. Where had she found the time to do so much, unbeknownst to him? He pulled absently at his forelock, his heart swelling large in his chest, as full realization of her generous thoughtfulness swept over him. He patted her shoulder again, less awkwardly.

"My Christmas thanks to you for all these prideful things,

Tenny. You sure 'nough honored me. And more thanks, too, for your just bein' here to make this such a wond'rous day. Nothin' has been so right down perfect since Ma—"

He turned abruptly toward the fireplace to hide the uncontrolled twitching that had suddenly attacked the corners of his mouth. The rattle of the poker clashing against the back of the fireplace drowned her answering cry of thankfulness for the richness of blessings that had been accorded them.

CHAPTER 11

It was almost the end of January when Rance woke up one morning to discover a sharp cutting wind blowing out of the southwest. It must have been blowing all night. Tops of the snowdrifts were already honeycombed to a depth of six inches. Everywhere the snow level had settled noticeably. He leaned his slim body against the door frame, gazing contentedly at the scene. The big thaw! The end of over two months' imprisonment in a white world. Man alive, how good it would feel to get his feet on bare ground once more!

"Rance Hardig, are you trying to turn this house into an icebox? I could feel that wind in the bedroom, with the door shut."

Rance looked back over his shoulder to see Tenny standing in the middle of the room. She was shivering noticeably. His glance drifted to the fireplace. What flames there were leaped wildly up the chimney, as though determined to take all their heat to the upper regions. He pulled the door shut reluctantly.

"Chinook wind!" he said briefly. "It's cuttin' the snow liken a cow mows grass. We'll have plumb naked ground 'fore we know it."

"Oh? What on earth is a Chinook wind?"

"Come see for yourself. It's a west wind that melts snow liken a fire melts butter. Something kinda peculiar to this here northwest country, it seems. I never met one 'fore, but somebody made mention of it to Pa when we were up at

Oregon City. This couldn't be anything but what the man bespoke of."

Tenny came to peer over his shoulder. He shoved the door partly open, so she could see the water streaming off the roof to stand in puddles about the icy yard.

"Will it take the snow all off, Rance?"

"It's hard to tell. Prob'ly depends on how long this blow lasts." He canted an ear at the wind sighing through the trees and whining around the chimney. "Should it hang on, liken it sounds to be fixin' for, the crick'll be runnin' bank full by mornin'. That means I'd be somewhat of an addle-pate, was I to not git my traps hauled in afore the flood muds 'em over, or something."

"You mean right away?"

"D'rectly. You kin be hottin' up some breakfast whilst I milk an' feed. Then I'll be set to go. There's no profit in tarryin'."

Nevertheless, Rance felt the urge for a bit of tarrying, as he made his way up the creek an hour later. With a full stomach and exercise stirring his blood, the day wasn't at all uncomfortable. The well-trodden trap-line trail afforded fairly easy walking, aside from the rather squashy surface of packed snow. Collecting the catch of muskrats, two mink, and a raccoon, and pulling up the precious traps at each set was done more or less automatically. His truant mind persisted in deserting the present for vagrant ramblings back over the snowbound months since Tenny came into his life. Despite the phenomenal cold and continued storms, it had been a good winter. His fur catch, hanging on the barn rafters, would assure a sizable grubstake for the summer ahead. The stock had all wintered well, Tenny was back to full health, and their Christmas had been a prideful thing to remember always. He guessed the whole thing was about as full of richness as any fair-minded body could ask for.

"Yes, sir," he told himself, "It's been a right handsome time all the way through. What few scaly edges showed up didn't cut scarce a ripple. And now, with springtime fixin' to break, it should be all the better—if anything could be better."

Tenny, busy with her housework, was meanwhile, enjoying similar reflections. Rescued from hopeless tragedy and death, as well as the near fatal pneumonia, the joy of just being alive and in good health was a miracle to make the heart throb with happiness. Being snatched out of an unpeopled wilderness, to find herself in this snug cabin was something that only God could have planned for a destitute orphan. Her eyes lingered momentarily on the split-log table and its two closely related benches, the cherrywood rocker and rawhide-bottomed chair, the big occasional chest and the ever cheerful fireplace, the commodious wooden dish trough, with its remarkable elderberry drainpipe, and the fine array of food bags swinging from the long ridgepole. What a haven of comfort and security to find oneself enveloped in so unexpectedly! It was almost like being touched by the wand of the fairy Godmother in *Cinderella.* Even the bitter cold and frozen drifts of snow had worked their magic in bestowing the long winter evenings of homemade games, reading aloud to each other, and knowing the soul-satisfying companionship that only unburdened seclusion could bring. The new buckskin dress and beautiful cedar chest were a part of it, made possible by the snowbound hours designed to focus Rance's attention on the coming Christmas. Was any living soul ever so fortunate?

She leaned over the handle of the brush broom, staring thoughtfully into the fire. "Some Hardig," she assured herself, "must certainly have been a high-class gentleman of a noble family. It may have been pretty far back, but I'll wager he wore silks and velvet and the king's armor, whoever he was. That kind of blood shows up for ever so many generations. Nothing else could make Rance what he is!"

Rance, however, banished the king's favorite to the outer darkness immediately after supper. "Grandpa came to America as a gunsmith's helper," he said, in answer to her eager question. "He married a tavern wench an' took out to folla the West. I reckon they lived in a lot of places, from what I gathered. Anyhow, Pa was birthed in Ohio, somewheres along the Muskingum. He found Ma down around Louisville, Kentucky. After a few more moves, they made it on to Missouri in time for me to be born. That was kind of a poor-boy section, where they took up a farm. Nothin' much came of it. So, after a while, Pa decided to look for the Promised Land out in the Oregon country, like a lot of us hoop-pole an' crabapple hill-folks were set on. Nope, the onliest noble blood in our family musta come from some overseer's gad a-flayin' the field hands."

"Well," she conceded, "it could have been farther back than your grandfather. There were plenty of knights and court gentlemen all through the ages. Your grandfather might easily have been a disowned son or a victim of persecution. History is full of such unfortunates."

"Uh-huh! And it's a heap fuller of scalawags and runaway servants. But I can't reckon it as a thing to fret over. No ancestors, big or little, are going to h'ist me up to a pinnacle at this late time."

"Good! Then I won't have to learn how to kowtow to a majesty." She wrinkled her nose at him. "I might fall on my face in the slush, anyway."

"Well, there'd be plenty to fall into this evenin'. I had sloppy going all the way in the last mile."

"Is it still thawing?"

"Yep. And stands to git more so. The wind's droppin', but there's rain in the air now. I felt a scad of sprinkles as I came in."

By mid-evening, the rain was fulfilling his predictions. Rance was pulling his freshly pelted furs onto stretching boards when he suddenly held up a finger for silence. Tenny straightened up to listen intently. Yes, that steady drowsy patter on the roof was rain, no mistake. And it was warming up as the wind died.

"Looks as how we might be afloat, come mornin'." He grinned good-naturedly.

It was a prime comfort to remember how Pa had been so persnickety about picking a building spot well up above high-water danger. He felt even better when he looked out the following morning to see the bank-full creek running rampant below the base of the knoll on which the buildings stood. Little streamlets were rushing down every declivity, as if in a hurry to deposit their burdens in the creek below. Around the house and barn, the matted grass and bare patches of earth were showing through the dwindling snow. And still it rained, that soft, cloying downpour so distinctive of the western Oregon country. Rance shoved Tenny back inside the door, following in her footsteps.

"Let's have some breakfast," he suggested. "Might be it'll slack off, so I won't have to play beaver gittin' to the barn."

"We should have left your hair on," Tenny laughed. "It would have been long enough by now to keep the rest of you dry."

He grinned, toying with his forelock. "'Twas that second cuttin', two weeks agone, that ruint things. I'd gained back enough to keep rain from goin' down my collar, but you would shear it just ahead of this needful time."

"Well, my efforts will at least keep you from looking like a drowned rat, every time you stick your head outdoors."

"I wasn't aimin' to stick it out in no rainfall liken this. A body might ketch his death of something. It's best to hover next the fire in such dang'rous times."

"It's a good thing you didn't feel that way when you were bringing me down off the mountain, last fall."

"There was no fire to cozen me up there." He flashed his infectious grin. "This cabin was the onliest place I knew to git warm."

She set the bowl of cornmeal mush down in front of him. "Old softy!" she mocked. "You might as well get at your eating. I think the rain is about to let up enough for you to be safe."

"Prob'ly just a-foolin', so's to ketch me out at the barn or somewheres. A body's never safe in temptin' providence."

Rance found, however, that providence was harboring no uncharitable intentions. By the time breakfast was over, the downpour had modified itself into a lazy drizzle. As he sloshed his way out to do the chores, he felt his nostrils lift to the scent of wet earth and thawed manure piled outside the barn. His outdoor senses told him that spring would not be long in coming. He wasn't sure whether or not he appreciated bidding goodby to winter. It had been such a pleasant time. All those long carefree evenings, the leisure of undemanding days, would have to suffer under the necessities of spring and summer work.

Moreover, an uninvited thought prodded him with the irritating reminder that his mind had been shirking Tenny's problem all these weeks. The ending of winter would mean open trails. And open trails would call for that long belated decision what to do about her. Rance scowled up at the sky, one hand straying to his forelock. He kicked an inoffensive clod through the barn doorway.

Doggonit! Why did unsettling things like that have to come sticking their heads up out of the dark, when they had been sleeping all winter? Still, it was pretty early yet. It might freeze up again, or let down another big snow. Anyhow, there wouldn't be any decent traveling for quite a spell. He guessed he'd have plenty of time to study on it, before the time came.

Meanwhile, this milder weather would be good for her, let her be outside more and kind of toughen up some after the long stretch of indoor housing. Mayhaps he could even help her out with that, by doing a mite of the housework, so she'd have more spare time to traipse around with him. A good build-up in strength would rightly make her better fitted for whatever he decided to do with her, later on. Yes, sir, that was the most meanful reasoning right now. The rest would work itself out, give it a chance.

He found "Oh! Susanna" on his lips, eager to help shove bothersome decisions into the background. The tune carried him through the rest of his chores, blissfully unaware that the fates were already conspiring on schemes of their own to take over both his and Tenny's affairs.

As if to lend aid in easing weighty problems, the springlike days came on apace. The remaining snow, honeycombed to the unfrozen ground by the Chinook wind, disappeared in a matter of days. Ankle-deep mud slowly dried under sunny skies and the lengthening hours of daylight. No longer was it necessary to keep the cabin door closed during midday hours or stable the animals every night. Tenny's lilting voice filled the clearing with song on the least pretext, while Rance's message to "Susanna" was a clarion call at dawning and a benison at night.

It was in mid-February that he began eyeing the patch of brush that hid the east end of the garden from the house. Grubbing it out would increase the size of the garden, as well as giving him a clear passage between the two places. The creek had gone down to normal size. Most of the bottom-land mud was solid enough to insure dry footing while still retaining the undersurface moisture that would allow easy removal of the tangled roots. Now would be the time to accomplish the task, before more pressing work claimed his attention. He sharpened up the grubbing hoe after supper that evening.

"Could I be of any help to you with that clearing?" Tenny asked, glancing back over her shoulder from where she was putting away the supper things. "I could perhaps pile and burn brush, or something."

"No, I reckon not. It's too hefty a job for a girl. 'Sides, I can't see why you should, when you've already got a heapin' plenty to keep you busy around the cabin."

"Wel-l-ll, I thought we might make a trade. I've been wishing ever since the weather turned nice that you might find time to do some little extra jobs for me. I'd be glad to help you in some way, to make up for the time you'd lose doing them."

"Oh, so that's it. And just what have you been honin' to have me do?"

She leaned back against the table, resting her weight on both arms slanted behind her. Her full lips curved in the smile that sent the familiar wrinkles climbing up the sides of her nose. Thoughtful seriousness widened the brown eyes.

"My greatest wish," she said slowly, "is to have some kind of a window in the bedroom. I don't like to complain, but you know how dark it is in there. All this sunshine outside makes it seem darker and gloomier than ever. A window something like the one in this room would be wonderful. Then I could do up the work in there without having to light a candle or leave the outside door open."

She paused to slant a sidewise glance at Rance, bent silently forward in the rawhide-bottomed chair. All his attention seemed riveted on the grubbing hoe in his lap. Her lips tightened in a sharp line. She half turned away, then straightened her shoulders with a brusque shrug.

"Second," she went on with crisp determination, "I truly need some kind of a clothes-drying rack out in the yard. Washdays are getting to be a trial, with things falling or blowing off the bushes onto the muddy ground. I thought you might manage to put up some poles, or something, that would be more reliable. I really need a clothes basket, too, but that can wait. Or maybe I could make that myself, if you would show me how to weave willows."

"Hm-m-m!" Rance came slowly out of his abstraction. "That's a notion worth yokin' some thought to," he said. "Such a thing plumb got past me. But now't you mention it, I kin see how another winda would work to lighten up the whole place. And it would be no big chore to chop a hole in the bedroom wall. And fixin' up a clo'es rack for dryin' would be easy, too; skin some willa saplin's to put up atween a post an' them two big trees. Yes, sir, that's a prime idea. We might even rig up some way to keep the clo'es from slippin' off the poles."

"Why, that would be simply wonderful!" She clapped her hands in mixed delight and relief. "But I still think you should let me help you with something in return for so much effort."

"Well, mayhaps. We'll see. It might be you could help fire the brush, once I git it piled, if you're so set about bein' beholdin' to me."

Her body stiffened tautly. To have her offer of help meet such an uncompromising attitude was like a slap in the face. She bit down hard on her lip.

"Beholding has nothing to do with it, Rance Hardig. You know that as well as I do. And you needn't worry about me wanting to help you again. If we can't help each other, there is nothing more to be said."

"Mayhaps you're right," he admitted. "But your work around the cabin is a high plenty for your share. There's no call for you to fret about takin' on my chores, too."

"But, Rance, that—"

"No buts about it. And you'll git your window." His mouth closed with a snap.

Tenny turned sharply on her heel, slamming the bedroom door behind her. Bafflement stiffened her back and set her feet down with solid thumps at each step. She had felt unaccountable moments of edginess creep into her mind of late. It was becoming increasingly easy to quarrel. No doubt it was only touches of that cabin fever that Rance had mentioned afflicting some people after long confinement together, but who wouldn't get cabin fever from living with such everlasting stubbornness? Rance Hardig, she concluded, must have taken lessons from that ornery stinker of a Buck mule!

The actual fruits of this refusal to let her help with the clearing did not, however, appear until a few days later. She declared afterward that the Lord must have made him bull-headed on purpose. There was no other way to account for the fact that her forced stay at the cabin was the only thing that saved both of them.

CHAPTER 12

There had been no hint of trouble the day the Indians came. Peaceful quiet reigned over the valley, drowsing lazily under the mid-afternoon sun. A vagrant breeze was sifting down from the high peaks, lightly ruffling the feathers of the flock of towhees busily arguing with a pair of whisky-jacks over the crumbs Rance had scattered after his return from dinner. The old woodpecker had resumed his drumming on the hemlock snag. A pair of early mallards quacked their approval of a choice find farther up the creek. The stream itself sang its gay undertones of springtime delights as it danced over the pebbly bottom.

Rance was bent over, prying at a stubborn root. He heaved irately on the grub-hoe handle. It reminded him of Tenny's stiff-necked standoffishness these last few days, her acting like he wasn't even fit to talk to. An angry mutter formed against his lips, waiting for a breathing spell.

He heaved again, letting his breath run out with a grunt of relief as the root at last came free. Half straightening, he shoved it aside with his grub-hoe. It was then that his eyes caught a flicker of movement beside the uncleared willows below him. He jerked himself suddenly erect, a stifled cry clogging his throat.

The two Indians were no more than thirty yards away, loping on moccasined feet around the elbow of brush. They had already seen him. No doubt they had been watching for some time, waiting for an opportune moment. It was evident, by their paint-daubed grins, that they were hoping to be on top of him before he realized their presence. The leader already had an arrow fitted to his bowstring. His companion's spear was poised in a dark, sinewy hand.

Rance wasted no time. One glance was enough. His rifle, left leaning against a stump, was too far away to do him any good. He sucked in his breath, jumping sidewise and ducking low as he moved. His feet struck the ground in a racing stride. The hundred yards up to the cabin seemed to stretch out interminably. His feet felt the added weight of clinging mud donated by the stump hole.

On he ran, his zigzag dodging stealing precious yards from his progress. The savage yells behind him seemed to mock his labored breathing. An arrow hissed past his left shoulder. Another drove into the ground beside him. One foot struck a rounded rock, throwing him off stride for a second. He caught his footing and raced on, his breath whistling in great, ragged gasps. The yells were coming closer. He was only halfway to the cabin. The Indians must be gaining fast, but he didn't dare waste the split second needed to look behind.

He was in the middle of a sidewise leap, when something struck his thigh a stunning blow. He spun half around and went to his knee. One outflung hand drove into the dirt, levering him partly upright a moment later. It was then that he saw the black obsidian point jutting out on the end of its shaft, a finger's breadth beyond his leg. Bright trickles of blood were already dripping from the grooved shaft. Could he make it on? He must! Tenny couldn't be left alone! He lurched ahead.

But the injury had cost him dearly. The running feet sounded to be almost upon him. Another arrow hissed past him. The thrown spear flashed by his head. He flinched instinctively against its breath fanning his ear. Mist fogged his eyes, making the cabin sway crazily, as though dancing farther away.

Baroom! The crashing echoes rolled across the clearing like a clap of thunder. Rance's eyes lifted. He couldn't mistake the roar of that old cap-lock shotgun. He half saw Tenny in the doorway, the gun still cuddled against her cheek. At the same instant, the weapon bellowed its wrath again, vomiting smoke and fire, as from the mouth of a vengeful dragon. Rance swung his head back over his shoulder to see the leading Indian sprawled in the grass, his head half blown away. His companion was shortly behind, writhing like a brown snake between two half-buried boulders. Even as he looked, the painted marauder stiffened suddenly and went limp.

Rance hobbled on up to the cabin. He leg hurt fiercely, but he guessed the arrow had missed the bone. Otherwise, it wouldn't have come on through. Then the wound wouldn't be too bad. Just a flesh injury! He went on. Thank God Tenny hadn't been down by the creek! That was the only thing that had saved them both.

He found her leaning weakly against the door frame. The gun hung limp in her shaking hands. Her eyes looked big as saucers in the white face.

"I—I killed them!" she muttered tonelessly. "I couldn't help it. They—they—"

"You saved my life, Tenny," he broke in. "And prob'ly yours, too. They were a-fixin' to murder us both, the bloodthirsty damn savages! Just liken they did Pa an' Ma an' your folks. You're a hero for stoppin' 'em, twice over!"

"I don't feel so. It's awful to kill humans."

"They're not human, the dirty butchers!"

"I know. But—but—" She smiled tremulously. "There was nothing else to be done. Anyhow, it's sort of a score against what they did to my folks. And they'd have had you in another minute. Your falling and—why, you're wounded!"

"Only through the meat." He reached down and snapped off the stone point, then turned his back to her. "Grab that shaft and yank it out! One big heave, 'thout no slackin' off!"

"But, Rance, I can't! It will hurt you so—"

"Do what I say! Haul it out 'fore it hurts worse!" He grabbed the door frame to brace himself. "Pull hard an' keep pullin'. You gotta; I can't reach it."

"All right." She reached tentatively for the shaft. "I don't know. I—I—"

"Shut up an' git it out! Now!" His voice was like a whiplash. "Don't be a pure fool! I can't stand here with this misery all day."

Tenny's eyes clouded with tears at the almost savage rebuke. All right, if he wanted more punishment, he could have it! With eyes closed and lips a thin line, she clasped the shaft with both hands and literally threw herself backward.

She landed on her back a yard behind him. The blood-soaked shaft had slid free with unexpected ease. She gulped for breath, dropping the reddened arrow as she struggled to her feet. A mixture of mirth, dismay, and embarrassment twisted at her face. Laughter fought with unshed tears to leave her wringing her hands in helpless confusion.

"It's out!" she said inanely. "All the way."

"Good girl! You shore 'nough make a prime hand when I need help. I dunno how I'd ever make out without you."

He glanced down at the blood puddling around his foot. "Now, if you're up to a mite more help, you might git me some soft pads an' bandages. I kin tend the doin' up whilst you swab out the gun. And, oh yes, put a spoon of sugar on each pad, then soak 'em with turpentine. That's the best cure for fresh cuts."

Half an hour later, he came out of the leanto to find her cleaning the shotgun. Tears had cut white furrows down her muddy cheeks, leaving the brown eyes still clouded with mist. She laid down the cleaning rod and bit her lips.

"Leg feels fine now," he said. "I'm shore sorry about rawhidin' you so rough, liken I did. It was just that these things have to be done sudden-like, whilst the hurt's still half numb. And I'm still praisin' you for that man-size bit of rescuin'. Right prideful of you, I am. I'd 'a' been rubbed out for sure, otherwise."

"Thanks, Rance! I'm g-glad I was of some help, at last."

"You're a plumb pardner, all the way. I won't be slightin' your wants agin."

"That makes me very happy. But are you sure you are all right now?"

"Sartin! There's nothin' to fret about now. Good clean cuts liken that heal up easy. The main thing is we've still got our hair."

He lifted the shotgun from her hands and reached for the powder horn. It was a comfortable feeling to know he had jarred her out of maybe going to pieces, after the killing and pulling the arrow out. She'd had him right purely worried for a while.

"I'll just refodder this weapon," he went on, "in case you find it needful to save my hide agin, sometime. Pa allus held that readiness an' rightfulness were the twins that won the most battles. That was something you proved out right smart today."

"Thanks!" She lifted to her feet, practicality overcoming

her shaken nerves. "Now you'd better go lie down and rest that leg." She deftly transferred the gun from his hands to the deer-horn rack, before he realized what she was doing. "It won't help things any to stand around or walk on it."

"Oh, I'm not that bad off. It's just a flesh cut. The hurtin' left off soon's you yanked out that arrow shaft. Anyhow, I've gotta git rid of them two—"

"That pair won't hurt anything if left for a while." She shoved him unceremoniously down in the cherrywood rocker. "Your job is to take care of that leg. I don't want an invalid on my hands. We'll see about doing something with the Indians later on. Maybe tomorrow, if your wound stops bleeding and there are no complications."

"But I tell you I—"

"And I'm telling you! We'll see how you feel tomorrow. For the present, you stretch that leg out and keep it quiet. I'll do the milking and get us some supper after a while."

She closed the argument by disappearing into the bedroom, leaving Rance to search futilely for words. She returned a moment later with one of the feather pillows off the bed. Laying it lengthwise of the log bench, she dragged the latter around in front of the rocker.

Rance grinned wryly as she motioned him to lift his leg. Treating him like a plumb cripple already! Yet he was forced to admit that the puckering pain eased off somewhat as soon as the bench slid into position and he let the leg's weight down onto the pillow. He might as well humor her, he reckoned. Being let to feel helpful seemed to pleasure her a lot. Probably helped to keep her mind off the shooting, too. He fingered his forelock, leaning restfully back in the rocker. He guessed that laying off a few hours wouldn't hurt much, the afternoon being already nigh spent, anyhow.

"I'll make it up tomorra," he consoled himself.

Morning, however, aligned itself with Tenny's urging that he spend another day of quiet. The sharp arrow had shashed a clean cut through the fleshy part of his thigh, halfway between hip and knee. It had missed both the bone and big muscles. There seemed nothing to worry about. Still, with the shock worn off, any exertion or sudden movement of the leg made him wince against the stab of pain. Moreover, he had had a restless night, torn between uneasy sleep and nagging throb of the wound. It was with rather self-conscious relief that he awoke late to find Tenny had milked old Brockle, carried in the day's wood, and was now putting breakfast on the table. With his leg stretched out on the padded bench, he was content to follow her advice and stay indoors the rest of the day.

"I reckon a bread and milk poultice over each end of that hole might be a tol'able help," he suggested, settling back in the rocker after breakfast. "Especially if you could dig out some moldy bread. The worth of this sugar an' turpentine has done used itself up."

"But why moldy bread?"

"I dunno. Ma allus held it was best to drag out any poison, 'sides doin' a power of healin'."

"How should I fix it?" She came out of the bread box with two mold-speckled crusts. "I never heard of such a thing."

"Well, it allus seemed to work for Ma. She claimed the mold helped somehow. Her way was to heat the milk, then soak the bread in it. Make kind of a mush of it, she would, afore bindin' it on the hurt. I r'member from her usin' it on me how it would draw bad matter out of a cut an' keep the place open for rightful healin'."

In truth, Ma's remedy seemed to have lost none of its potency under alien hands. Rance slept much better that night.

He was also able to work some of the stiffness out of his leg the following day, after a few hours of treatment under fresh poultices.

"It shore feels better," he exulted, after a short turn about the yard. "There's scarce any of that bad hurtin' left. It seems you're nigh on to bein' as good a doctor as Ma was."

"Maybe, when I have you to tell me how. It's all new to me. Old Dr. Spiegel always tended our ailments back home. I stayed clear of such things."

"Well, you shore 'nough seem to be gifted thataway. The way things work for you, I'd swear you was born to it."

Tenny's back was turned, hiding the sudden bright flush mounting high in her cheeks, but her half-audible "H-m-m!" trilled a note of pleasure as she bent lower over the dish trough. She set the iron cooking pot back on the hearth, standing for a moment with hands braced on the trough edges. Her eyes thoughtfully followed the dishwater gurgling out through the elderberry stem.

Standing thus, Rance's gaze was unwittingly drawn to the nest of black curls cuddled snugly against the back of her neck. All he could think of was a border of black lace framing the buckskin dress collar. It made a mighty sightful thing to look at, he thought, especially when she turned so the light from the window struck it just right.

If she had that bedroom window, now, there'd like as not be a good light on it, no matter how she turned. He tugged at his forelock. Seeing as how he'd promised to make a window, that would be a right proper thing for him to tinker at while it was still awkward for him to finish the grubbing. Yes, sir, a body lucky enough to have such a partner to do for him, when he ran afoul of something, should cotton to her wants as much as he rightly could. And chopping out a window hole wouldn't take any special leg work. Tomorrow would be a likely day for it, if his hurt kept easing off anyway fair-like.

And the leg did feel much easier the next morning. A few turns about the house limbered it up without much trouble. Fresh poultices had abolished nearly all of the pain of movement. With most of his weight resting on a length of fireplace wood, propped under his hip, he found he could swing the axe in comparative comfort. Before noon, Tenny's glad cry met the glow of sunlight bursting suddenly into the bedroom.

Rance whistled a few bars of "Oh! Susanna." It was mighty nice to see how the new opening seemed to make the whole cabin more cheerful. He guessed he would enjoy it as much as she did, as soon as he got the log-ends squared up with Pa's handsaw, and a shutter made.

Another morning found the leg responding with only a minor show of stiffness. He guessed that buckling down to that window job had done it a power of good. More of the same would no doubt keep it coming along without any further trouble. His glance drifted across the still figures lying halfway down the slope. Might as well saddle up the gray mare and drag them away back in the timber, somewhere. Buzzards and wolves would take care of the rest of it, in a short spell. And what better did they deserve? It was a right good feeling to know he had chalked up another score against the tribe that slaughtered his and Tenny's folks. It was just too bad there weren't more of them to drag off.

He was back at the cabin in time for dinner, his grisly task finished. He guessed she had noticed what he was doing; there was no use talking about it. Tenny's little stack of freshly washed clothes offered a handy diversion. It was also a potent reminder of the promised drying rack. One finger strayed to his forelock. A few slender willow poles, he concluded, supported by the two trees west of the house and a cross-arm on one post, should make a real substantial rack. That clump of willows out back of the barn would be easy to get at and the peeling could be done sitting down. He limped out the door to get his axe.

"That's just perfect!" Tenny exclaimed later, running her eyes along the freshly peeled poles outlined against a setting sun. "I never really expected anything so fancy. And having one end on that post will give good sun-drying for anything that needs it."

"I'm proud it suits you." Rance's face reflected his pleasure as he lashed one end of the last pole to the cross-arm on the post. "I'll try to rustle you some little springy limb-forks right soon, gouged out to fit the poles for keepin' the clo'es from skiddin'."

"You think of everything, don't you? And I thank you ever so much for making my washdays that much easier. Having this along with my wonderful new window really completes my happiness. I think you deserve a full day's holiday tomorrow, with maybe a raisin pie for a special treat."

The squirrel chittered its approving encore from its perch on the farthest clothes pole.

Rance's holiday, however, did not materialize until two days later. It came, he said with a slow grin, as sort of a reward for the window shutter he had made for her bedroom. Tenny had stretched a piece of wet deer hide over the opening, while he rived out enough cedar shakes to cover the whole window. Operated by thongs, like he had devised for the other window, they could enjoy the light in good weather, while assuring themselves of full security against anything that might attack from the outside.

The attack came to test their work the next morning.

They awoke to gloomy skies and a raw southwest wind. A wall of mottled black clouds was building up over the Coast Range. Shortly before noon, the cabin suddenly echoed to the blast of lashing spring rain. Rance grinned across the fireplace as Tenny filled their plates with sizzling steaks speared from the heavy iron spider. He cocked an eye at the roof and hugged himself significantly with both arms. Tenny set the pan of meat down to smile back at him. Memory of the shut-in winter twined their minds into a single thought. This cabin was their haven and security, no matter what came. No warning of the elements or savagery of nature could harm them inside their cozy sanctuary.

"It's nice to be home," Rance said lightly. "A body could git a real maulin', was he caught out in this."

"A home," Tenny added, "is the most wonderful thing in the world, regardless of what might be outside."

Something in her voice pulled Rance's eyes wider. He turned to stare into the fire. She sounded almost as though the cabin was as much hers as his. And that she wasn't nowise fixing to look further for a home. The thought gave him the queer feeling of balancing himself on a slim pole while crossing a deep gorge. His fingers reached instinctively for the straw-colored forelock.

CHAPTER 13

It rained for three days, a steady drumming downpour. Winter was having its last belated fling. Cold driving rain slashed at the naked bodies of cottonwood and willows. The dull green boughs of fir and pine dripped soddenly under the weight of drenching torrents. Overhead, a gray formless blanket billowed down to treetop level, seemingly in momentary danger of being torn loose from the sky by the very weight of unshed water dragging it earthward. Gone were the mounting heights of timbered ridges and snow-capped peaks, swallowed up by the engulfing monster which drove its breath through every crack and crevice, while clawing at the valley slopes with shapeless fingers of fog. Nearer at hand, the creek growled and roared between its flooded banks, its heavy bass voice drowning out the merry tinkle of myriad streamlets rushing downhill through every depression. Old Brockle mooed her plaint from the meager protection of the shed. The gray mare pawed listlessly at a growing puddle in the barn doorway, while the Buck mule unperturbedly nosed the manger for overlooked wisps of hay.

"Are you sure you shouldn't be building an ark instead of that hot-weather hat?" Tenny stirred the fire to a brighter blaze. "I am beginning to feel like a second Mrs. Noah already."

Rance shrugged over the piece of soaked rawhide he was stretching over a head-shaped block of wood pegged to a plank base. He secured it carefully in place with a cord tied around its base, then flared the edge out brim-shaped on the plank. Not until he had weighted down the brim and set it to shrink-dry itself into shape beside the fire did he look up.

"I reckon it'll stop, give it time," he said, flipping a careless hand toward the roof. "It allus has."

"That's not saying it always will. This may be the exception. At least, it acts that way."

"Just like a man hittin' his thumb with a hammer: you'd think he's never going to quit swearin'. Yet he's bound to run down 'fore he starves to death."

"All right, smarty!" The laugh wrinkles were beginning to run up her nose. "We'll see tomorrow. If this storm quits swearing, I'll admit you are right."

"Like as not it will, just to keep you from takin' off for Mount Ararat." He tossed the scraps of rawhide into the fire and stretched the stiffness out of his cramped leg. "Now't I've got that job outa the way, 'twouldn't surprise me nowise to see it fair off 'most any time. It was prob'ly just connivin' to keep me housebound till I got the hat finished."

And, as if nature had indeed conspired to shape his affairs, the sun broke forth like some great, golden galleon in an endless blue sea the following morning. Opening the door to its growing light, he leaned against the wall to watch the storm climb the mountains to the east with gigantic strides. In its wake, tall spirals of steam rose from the warming earth to stand like shimmering ribbons against the sky. A soothing breeze whispered its way out of the southwest. The old woodpecker was back at work on the dead snag, his cheerful pounding an accolade to the drumming of a blue grouse in some distant thicket.

"Oh! Susanna" accompanied Rance on his way to the

barn, until put to rout by the Buck mule's reedy voice proclaiming its belief in spring's arrival. Old Brockle bawled her accompaniment while she studied the steaming hillside with a wistful gaze. Even the gray mare tried to copy the heifer calf's pirouetting course across the corral, only to strike a slick spot that left her sitting on her tail like a disgruntled dog. Nothing could escape the intoxicating breath suffusing the valley. Rance felt its insidious lure seep into his veins as memory of his promise to help Tenny with her churning hurried him through the milking.

"Let's go for a walk this afternoon," Tenny proposed, suddenly pausing midway of the butter-making. "This beautiful sunshine will soon have things pretty well dried off. And we needn't go far. Just anywhere, or anything, out in the open would be a delight after these last three days cooped up inside the cabin. It won't take long to get dinner out of the way."

"That suits me. It's too muddy for any field work, and the crick's still got my brush grubbin' drowned out. A smidgin of fresh air an' sunshine would likely profit us both. I misdoubt it will be overdry that soon, but we can come back, should our feet start dissolvin'."

"That's the way I feel. So where shall we go?"

"Anywheres that pleasures you." He swung his long legs straddle of the bench and sat down. "Might mosey up an' see how that big beaver dam weathered the flood, or whatever you'd like."

"The dam it is then. I've wanted to see that place ever since you first told me about it." She was already hurrying dinner onto the table. "It must be pretty, if this flood hasn't destroyed it."

"Well, we'll find out. 'Tain't far up there."

They ate quickly. Tenny complained that she was too

excited to bother with much food, anyway. She hurriedly cleared up the table while Rance took his rifle down from the deer-horn rack. A single glance assured him it was properly loaded and capped. He slung the powder horn and bullet pouch over one shoulder. His knife rested comfortably in its sheath at his left hip.

"We might see some fresh meat along the way," he explained casually.

Tenny nodded. Then suddenly: "Oh, your new hat!" She reached for the recent creation, only yesterday removed from its drying block to hang on a wall peg. "This is a perfect day to initiate it. I'll bet even the beavers will applaud—if they aren't all washed away."

Rance ducked his head to let her set it in place. He instinctively shifted it to a more comfortable position, as all men have done since hats were first invented. The soft buckskin strip Tenny had sewn in for a sweatband gave it a most agreeable fit. He grinned self-consciously into Pa's little shaving mirror that she held up before his face. Not too poorly, he decided, for a first job of hat-making. One hand shoved it more to the back of his head, trying the effect of the brim turned partly up. He grinned his pleasure and stepped out into the sunlight.

"Very handsome!" Tenny smiled her approval, closing the door behind them. "And a piece of work to be proud of."

He nodded his thanks, moving off toward the creek trail. Her words made him feel warm all over, though he found himself hoping he didn't show it. It was enough to have just his own private self thinking about how lucky he was to have a partner like Tenny, all full of praiseful words and a feel for make-do things a body tried to contrive.

This sense of well-being grew steadily under the lazy springtime breeze and warming sun. The white buds of pussy willows were beginning to open above the surge of muddy creek water. Pine squirrels chittered saucily overhead. Quail and grosbeaks scratched busily for seeds hidden beneath the tattered remnants of fallen leaves. A raucous blue jay disputed their passage until the last instant, as they rounded a sharp bend in the trail. A big-eyed rock rabbit scurried back to its winter lair among some tumbled boulders, as a foraging mink slid gracefully into the water. Tenny was everywhere. Now she stepped aside to fasten her eyes on a daring trillium nodding shyly in the sheltering niche of a rock face. A moment later, she was staring skyward at a pair of golden eagles floating on motionless wings above the creek, their eyes probing for any flood victim washed up on the bank. And over all hung the drowsy hum of insects and prospective life awakening from its chrysalis beneath the sheltering grass laid down by autumn frosts. It was a time for youth to sing its pleasures; a time for age to renew its faith; a time for nature to rejoice in a world newborn.

Tenny carelessly swung the slatted sunbonnet Ma had left hanging above the chest of drawers. Her eyes were as bright as the tune that bubbled from her lips. The skipping feet were no less nimble than those of the ground squirrel which dashed suddenly across her path.

"Isn't it heavenly?" she cried above the rumbling of the creek. "All of it, the sun, the air, the smell of things coming to life, the—the—oh, just everything!" She flung her arms in the air and spun elflike down the trail.

Rance's lips curved in a slow grin as he tugged at his forelock. It was sure right down nice to hear somebody put into words the things he had been feeling all along. And nobody but Tenny could have worded them so purely tune-like. Her voice, her actions, seemed to be a part of everything around them, liken she might have been birthed among the wood spirits themselves.

"It's shore a most amazin' day," he said impulsively, the words coming without conscious thought. Surprise and something akin to awe tinged the wonder of discovering the soul of magic in an everyday world. "Yes, sir, it's right uncommon handsome. A body couldn't come up with another day to match it in a month's ride." He seized her free hand to point out a tiny sun-drenched, parklike island surrounded by towering fir trees. Steam rose from the warming earth to join with the sun in painting a miniature rainbow against the green foliage. "Now ain't that the sightliest thing you most ever laid eyes to?"

Added pleasure awaited them at the beaver dam. It was an immense structure, raising the creek body a full eight feet to create a pond upwards of a hundred yards long. Rance judged it to be the mother colony of the neighborhood. He had, therefore, taken care to leave plenty of breeding stock for repopulating the valley. Pa always held that a man greedy enough to eat his seed for next year's crop had about as much to look forward to as a sow that ate her pigs. It was with a sense of personal achievement that he viewed the uninjured dam in connection with his plans for future fur harvests.

Tenny laughed her delight at this first sight of the dam and pond. It fitted Rance's description perfectly, or would, as he said, as soon as the water went down enough to expose the border of cattails and cove full of waterlilies. The dappled shadows of cottonwood and alder were as entrancing as the sheet of water plunging over the length of intertwined tree branches, rocks, and mud. Her first thought was what an ideal place it would be for lazy dreaming on a quiet summer afternoon.

Lost in pleasant abstraction, she was only roused to realities by Rance's sharp exclamation. He was staring down at the water below the end of the dam. She stepped over beside him.

"What is it?" she asked.

"Thought for a minute it was a man." He moved forward for a better view. "The wind keeps shiftin' the shadows of—"

He broke off in mid-sentence to start loping down the slope. "It is a man!" he flung back over his shoulder.

Tenny was right behind him. Her eyes searched the tricky shadows along the bank. Then she saw it, too, almost awash in the edge of the creek, under the overhanging bank below the dam. There could be no mistaking that sprawled figure.

Rance slid to a stop, gazing down at the water-soaked man below him. The fellow had evidently been the victim of an accident while crossing the dam. One ragged pant leg was bloodstained half its length. Another brownish smear mottled the shoulder and sleeve of the jacket. Bloody streaks disfigured one side of his face, running down from the dark hairline.

Rance moved forward a step, then reared abruptly back in his tracks. Anxious concern vanished suddenly under a mask of venomous hatred. His lips pulled back in a savage snarl as the huddled figure, roused by his approach, lifted its head a trifle to gaze blankly around. One black braid, freed by the movement, snaked its way up over the bloody sleeve to frame the mahogany-colored face. Rance's thumb fumbled for the rifle hammer as he jerked up the weapon.

Caught by the movement, the Indian's eyes swung upward to meet his. Wordlessly and without expression, the face stared back at him. Rance caught the fleeting impression of a trapped lynx cat crouched back the length of the trap chain, waiting unflinchingly for whatever might come. He raised the rifle slowly to his shoulder, carefully centering his sights on the bloodstained face. His finger curved tensely around the trigger.

CHAPTER 14

"No!"

Tenny threw herself headlong at him. One outflung hand knocked the rifle barrel sidewise. The sudden attack staggered Rance. Too late, he felt the thrust of her hand on the barrel exert its pull against his crooked trigger finger. The rifle's report boomed hollowly in his ears, as its leaden ball skittered harmlessly across the creek.

"What in tarnation—?" He caught his balance to glare his wrath at the girl. "Are you plumb loony? What'd you think you—?"

"I couldn't let you murder a helpless creature like that."

"It's just another lousy redskin. Prob'ly sneakin' in to burn us out or bushwhack one of us."

"Well, by his looks, I don't think you need worry about that. He appears to be more dead than alive."

"What of it? He's an Injun, ain't he? And why all this sudden sympathy for one of the red devils, after what they done to your folks, an' mine, an' come nigh onto doin' for me?"

"That wasn't the work of this fellow."

"'Twoulda been, was he there. They're all alike."

"They are no such thing."

"Who gave you all that knowin' talk?"

"I didn't need any telling!" Growing anger reddened her cheeks and raised her voice. "Anybody with wits enough to tell which way is up could see that this fellow is not one of the Rogues."

"A lot you know about it!"

"I'm not a headstrong idiot. I can still see both sides of a millstone in broad daylight. As much cause as I have to hate Indians, I despise the killing of them without reason. If you could think of anything but cold-blooded murder, you could see that this is only a boy, probably innocent of any hostile intentions, and definitely different from any of the Indians with whom we've had trouble."

"Well, I'm not chancin' anything." He was pouring fresh powder into his rifle. "An Injun's an Injun, an' better off dead."

"Just like all the whites are the same, I suppose?" She stepped back to flash a cold-eyed stare. "Which would put you and those prospectors you were telling me about in the same class. Is that it?"

"Well this—this is dif—"

"Exactly! The shoe pinches when you try it on yourself. Now let me tell you, Rance Hardig, I've suffered as much as you have. And I've killed men to save further suffering, the same as you. But I am not going to be a party to the murder of an innocent cripple, simply because he belongs to another race."

She was already running toward where the Indian lay, still staring at them with blank passivity. "You'd better go read your Bible again!" she threw back over her shoulder.

Rance pulled at his forelock while his mind grimaced slyly at his perplexity. What had twisted the grain in the girl, anyhow? This was a new Tenny, one he had never expected to see. He rammed a ball home in the rifle and started thoughtfully down the slope. And what did she mean about reading the Bible in connection with a prowling Indian? It just didn't make sense.

She was busy sponging the Indian's face with a wad of moss, when he slid down over the bank. The fellow had apparently lapsed back into unconsciousness. Or mayhaps he he was just pulling a whingding to fool them. You couldn't ever trust an Indian! He watched closely as she laid a restraining hand on the bloody shoulder, when the Indian stirred restlessly at his approach. Rance paused to stare at her, indignation struggling with puzzlement, as she looked around shyly, her anger apparently forgotten.

"You will have to help me," she murmured, her hands busy with the strap that held the Indian's bow case and arrow quiver in place. "This boy is seriously hurt. And hours of lying here freezing wet hasn't helped things."

"What you fixin' to do with him?"

"Take him to the cabin, where we can dry him out and dress his wounds. What else is there to do?"

"Knock him in the head! That is, unless you'd rather have him butcher us in our sleep. He's not packin' that knife an' tomahawk for fun. Experience shoulda taught you something about Injuns by now."

"It taught me enough about suffering that I won't leave this boy here to die." She straightened up and reached over to shake his arm. "Come on, forget about killing long enough to hunt up a couple of poles for a stretcher, while I gather grass and leaves to pad it. Please!"

Rance shook his head and turned away. Doctor an Injun? The whole idea was beyond all sense in thinking. He stared up the slope, his mind gazing blankly at a vision of having to live with a girl who had suddenly took full leave of her wits.

It was the faint "Please, Rance!" again in his ears that

brought him back around to face her. The soft brown eyes seemed to be holding back a flood of tears. They reminded him of the way Ma looked that time she had caught him trying to talk like a hooty owl over the last of Pa's medicine whisky when he was eight years old. He shrugged his shoulders resignedly. There seemed little you could do with a woman when she started greasing the ground under your feet. Still, the way she was taking on, and much as he hated to admit it, she mayhaps had the right of things in this deal, according to what a belated memory told him it said in the Bible book. Turning the other cheek should at least ease things off till they found out how bad the Indian was really damaged.

With a resentful grunt, he reluctantly set off around the flooded shoreline in search of the suitable poles. One backward glance disclosed Tenny up on the hillside, busily ripping out dead grass to cushion the injured body.

Half an hour later he was back, the two poles, across which he had lashed half a dozen small branches with strings of cedar bark, dragging behind him. He felt the worst of his disgruntlement fade out as he helped Tenny spread her armful of fir boughs over the crosspieces as support for the layer of grass. Crude though it was, it afforded a reasonably comfortable resting place for the Indian. His half-conscious grunt, as they lifted him gently onto the contrivance, was a mute signal of relief. The black eyes held an awakening glow of appreciation when Rance slung the bow and quiver across his own shoulder.

Getting the cumbersome weight up over the bank was something of a struggle, but they made it without upsetting their burden. The rest of the way was fairly easy. With Rance carrying the heavier front end, they made good time over the open trail.

Further encouragement came when they made their one stop for rest. The Indian showed a fair awareness of his surroundings. His mumbled, "Me, Joe. Good Indian," brought Tenny's head up with an "I told you so!" look. Rance grinned enigmatically. He guessed mayhaps the boy wasn't about to slaughter them, not right off, anyhow.

"You talk English?" he asked.

"Me know white man talk," came the hesitant reply. "Get from Lee's Mission School. Go much; three winter."

"Who are your people? What tribe you belong?"

"Me Calapooya. Calapooya long time white man friends. I come—com—" The voice faded out as its owner fell back limply on the litter.

"See!" Tenny exclaimed, her voice rising with gratified pleasure. "Now will you believe he is not one of those murdering Rogues?"

"Uh-huh! The Calapooyas are away up north, beyond the Umpquas. 'Tis said they're on the tame side." Rance's surrender was complete. His hand strayed to his forelock. He studied the again unconscious Indian for a moment, his ears turned to the labored breathing. "But if he ain't warrin', I'd be proud to hear what he's doin' 'way off down here."

"He will no doubt tell us as soon as he's able," Tenny said confidently. "I'll wager it has nothing to do with these scoundrels around here. I just hope he recovers to prove it."

The Indian, fortunately, seemed to be regaining some of his hold on life by the time they lifted him off the litter and laid him down before the fireplace. Rance hurriedly built up the fire while Tenny filled the big iron pot with water and hung it on the crane. The boy was responding visibly to the grateful warmth. His steady black eyes shone with thankfulness as he followed every move of his benefactors.

"You'll come out of it like a whirlwind, once we get you

dried out an' fed up," Rance said cheerfully. "Patchin' up these few rips won't take no time."

He turned abruptly to Tenny: "I'll rustle one of my blankets to be warmin' up, then git these wet duds off him whilst you round up some bandage stuff. Warmth's likely what he's perishin' for the most. He prob'ly fell off that dam whilst crossin' in the dark, sometime 'fore daylight—mayhaps earlier. That's a powerful long time to be drenched in ice water."

"It is indeed!" She turned toward the bedroom. "I'll find something. Perhaps my old petticoat will do. Nearly worn out, as it is, I've been thinking of making a new one out of your mother's other nightgown."

Rance grunted his agreement, as he stripped the Indian of his knife-and-tomahawk belt and ragged pants. The leg wound was more of a jagged tear than a deep cut. It had bled rather freely. Watery red drops still dotted the raw edges. It appeared to have been gouged by a sharp stick or broken tree limb, tearing through skin and flesh half-way down the thigh. It likely happened when he went off the dam, Rance thought. He slid the warm blanket beneath the brown legs, then folded it over to catch the fire's heat. He hoped that would counteract the sudden fit of shivering now agitating his patient.

The head wound was mostly a bad bruise edged by a Y-shaped cut. Rance put that down as collision with a rock that ended the eight-foot tumble. Perhaps it was this same rock that had smashed into the upper left ribs, laying open a long slash up to the shoulder blade. Removing the canvas jacket and faded plaid shirt had been something of a trial to both of them. Rance was sweating freely by the time he got the Indian laid back down and turned his attention to the wound. The shoulder appeared to be all right, nor was the cut dangerously deep, but his pressing fingers halted their search as the upper rib gave way under his touch. The Indian's sharp grunt of pain confirmed the suspicion of a broken rib. Rance pulled the blanket gently up over the naked shoulders and squatted back on his heels. One hand pulled thoughtfully at his forelock.

The cuts weren't particularly bad, he decided. Some soft pads coated with turpentine and sugar, for overnight, would be best. Then, in the morning, a liberal application of Ma's prime healing salve, made from a mixture of soap, sugar, vinegar, and sweet cream, should finish the job. There was never a better healer than that salve. It was lucky Ma had left a jar of it in the occasional chest.

The head injury, though, was different. Pa and Ma had both often remarked about what a cracked skull might lead to. This one might well be what caused the Indian's blacking-out spells. He ran an explorative finger around the discolored bruise. His breath hissed out with a relieved sigh when he could find no signs of a break. Like as not, it would take care of itself without any worry, if he heeded Pa's belief that the main thing was to trust Father Time and Mother Nature to work out a rightful healing.

Tenny's petticoat pads and bandages, fished out of the boiling water and coated with sugar and turpentine, seemed most soothing to the Indian. He gradually relaxed and quit his shivering under the warmth and friendly treatment. Even his eyes looked different, Rance thought, more like a spooky horse or dog that had decided only goodness could come from giving full trust to helping hands.

"Now what about that broken rib?" Tenny asked, when they had finished dressing the open wounds. "It doesn't seem like it should be allowed to wiggle around like that, with every move."

"It shouldn't. That's what's had me studyin' on it right smart. All I know is hearin' about a tight bandage 'round the chest for busted ribs. Might be that's all'ts needful; just something to keep the bone from shiftin' about."

"Something like this?" She held up a doubled length of petticoat bottom, perhaps eight inches wide. She gave it a demonstrative tug. "See it's still a real strong piece of goods."

"Dunno as we could do any better, an' that would be soft-like against his skin." He reached for the cloth and began working it down under the Indian's shoulder blades. "I wonder," he looked up, brows puckered in thought, "if it wouldn't be favorful for him to blow out all his wind, an' hold it, whilst we cinch this binder down? It seems liken that'd anchor things more; agin he refills his lungs, there'd be a tol'able amount of outward pressure to hold the rib snug aginst the binder."

"Why, I think that's a splendid idea, entirely reasonable." Tenny's set face dissolved in a quick smile. "How did you ever think of such a thing?"

"Fixin' up your crippled Injuns is enough to give a body all sorts of ideas. My latest one is for you to git what's left of our dinner stew on the fire. Then we kin fill this fella up with it as soon's we cinch his rib inta place. Nothin' will bring an Injun to life any quicker'n the prospect of a full belly."

"Just like a white man!" Her quick smile sent the wrinkles climbing up her nose. "What a wonderful equalizer is the human stomach!"

Rance abandoned the verbal battle with a shrug. It was no use trying to match wits with Tenny. Concealing a guarded grin, he carefully selected four slender pine splinters from the kindling basket and began sharpening them into tiny skewers with his knife. Then he started to explain, with signs, how the patient should expel his breath while the bandage was being applied.

The Indian nodded his understanding, after the second demonstration. "Blow out good," he grunted. "Yellow Hair fix."

"Fine, Joe! It won't take but a shake, if this smart pardner of mine'll hold the ends whilst I pin it."

Tenny was all seriousness again. Down on her knees, she pulled the overlapping ends of the cloth tight the instant she felt the chest relax beneath her fingers. Rance pinned them together with the prepared skewers a moment later. Both watched anxiously as the Indian sucked in an experimental breath. Everything held firmly. Full satisfaction followed. The Indian's breathing was normally rhythmic, with no evidence of serious physical discomfort.

"I'll make him a pallet alongside mine in the leanto, while you're hottin' up the soup," Rance said offhandedly. "That'll finish thawin' him out first rate. Then we kin skid him inta bed 'thout any trouble."

CHAPTER 15

The Indian improved rapidly. His head injury cleared up within a few days, leaving him rational and bright-eyed. The brown jar of homemade salve was healing the open wounds with all the magical efficiency for which it was famed. Even the broken rib seemed to be knitting satisfactorily. Its owner denied any particular pain from it, so long as he moved with reasonable caution. When it began to itch aggravatingly, Rance decided the break was mending itself without complications.

The successful recovery provided food for much good-natured controversy. None of them would take the credit for it. Tenny vowed it was entirely due to Rance's doctoring; Rance swore it all came from her refusal to let him shoot the boy when he was first found. The Indian, who clung to his mission name of Joe, insisted that his two white friends were equally responsible for having saved his life. They, he said, in his halting English, had been both father and mother, working as one to bring his spirit back to his body. He would have nothing to do with the suggestion that his own strength played any part in the proceeding. They were all finally forced to accept Tenny's verdict of a three-way partnership under a common flag.

"We all did the best we could," she said. "And everything worked to a happy conclusion. What's the difference how or why?"

"But I still claim the whole thing stems from your knockin' my gun cattywampus at the dam," Rance persisted.

"You would be as stubborn as a puppy with a root," Tenny countered. "But you shall not out-argue both of us. Anyway," she turned to Joe, sitting up in the cherrywood rocker, "we all know about these later happenings and what took place there at the dam. What I'd like to hear is the reason for your being down in this country. You never have told us about that."

Joe looked up, nodding. A pleased expression lighted his eyes. "Can tell," he said. "Skookum white friends bring Joe back from spirit world. Joe plenty happy. Now tell Yellow Hair an' white miss ever't'ing."

It was a long story, made longer by the search for English words, lengthy explanations in sign language, often obscure to white minds, and much rambling to bring all the details into proper focus.

As Rance summed it up afterward, the young Calapooya lived with his people, north across the divide from the Umpqua Valley. After three winters at the Lee Mission on the Willamette River, he had decided to continue on the white man's path. This led to his joining a party of white trappers up in the Middle Fork and McKenzie River region. He also did some meat hunting for the new settlers of the upper Willamette Valley. Both ventures increased his liking for the new way of life. This went on until the preceding fall.

His family had clung to the old life, roaming about the back country and following the ways of their ancestors. It was while on a visit to his family's lodge on the upper Willamette, during the big snow, that his older brother came home. The brother, more dead than alive from an old wound, collapsed in the arms of his father. He died soon afterward.

The story of how, with his two wives and small son, he had gone to visit some Umpqua friends was a thing of sadness. On their way home, shortly before the first frosts, they had swung up into the hills on the south side of the valley in search of berries. It was a fine year for berries. They hoped to gather a good supply for winter. And they met with gratifying success. In a short while, they had almost filled their rawhide parfleches for the journey home. Then, without warning, two white men made an unprovoked attack on their camp. With no pause for parley, they immediately started firing on the defenseless Indians. One woman fell over the fire, screaming horribly. The brother, his side torn open by a bullet, managed to escape into a brush-filled gulch. Further shots felled the other woman and boy before they could reach cover.

"How terrible!" sighed Tenny under her breath. "Such brutal savagery!"

Rance squeezed her hand, motioning for silence. His own emotion roiled the pit of his stomach. But he had to hear the rest of it.

The brother eventually dragged himself into a shallow cave, where he lived on berries and snared rabbits until his wound healed enough that he could travel to the lodge of his Umpqua friends. Most of his journey was through the first days of the big snow. Cold and exposure, coupled with his half-healed wound, almost finished him. It was only after many suns of tortured suffering in the friend's lodge that he found life enough to think of continuing on home. Again on his feet, he was deaf to reason. Against all the Umpqua's good advice, he was determined to go on north with his sad news. His weakened condition, however, proved no match for the ever recurrent storms and deepening snow.

By the time he staggered into his father's lodge, only a thin thread bound his spirit to his body.

The old father, Joe said, his eyes lifting over their heads, as though staring off into some great distance, was not strong enough to take the vengeance trail. Though still having known only eighteen winters himself, he was the only one left who was able to go in search of the enemy. In consequence, armed with his brother's description of the men who had so heartlessly murdered his inoffensive relatives, who had always been friendly with the whites, he had started his quest as soon as the snow was gone.

A short visit at the Umpqua village had netted him a little information about the many white men who had come to the Rogue River country in search of the yellow iron these last two summers. It was the Umpquas' belief that the murderers were of this company, some of whom were said to enjoy killing Indians, as they would *cultus* wolves. They were unable, however, to point to any individual ones who might be guilty. There had been no outside witnesses to the killings. The only thing the Calapooya could do was come on south, where most of the prospectors and miners congregated, in hopes of finding the ones described to him.

Joe felt sure that his medicine would eventually lead him to the murderers. He had a very strong spirit protector, he said, to whom he prayed every sunrise. Yet he knew he had to move carefully, mostly by night. The Umpquas had warned him about the white men who had come for gold. Many were more or less suspicious of all Indians since trouble first started with the Rogues. Some even went out of their way to kill any native they saw, just on general principles. All this made it extremely dangerous for any Indian to be seen by the barbarians who had invaded their country.

That was why the Calapooya waited for the cover of darkness when faced by any open country. The treeless meadowland along the creek was such a place. Ever aware of danger, he accordingly waited until shortly before daylight to attempt his crossing on the big beaver dam.

"And what happened at the dam?" Rance asked. "Did you meet an enemy?"

"Dam was enemy. Wet moccasin slip. Me fall 'gainst green stick of beaver sharpening. Fall hard on stick. Stick mak' plenty bend, then bite leg an' come back. Poof! Me hit rock under dam. Rock no kill. Water try drown. Joe's medicine strong. Get him on bank by'm by."

Rance glanced at Tenny. Both nodded in unison. The accident at the dam was as they had surmised. The rest made a clear picture. Rance pulled thoughtfully at his forelock as the Indian moved stiffly off to bed. He had spoken; there was no more to tell.

Rance watched Tenny follow his example, disappearing into the bedroom. Silently, he held his seat before the fireplace long after the cabin was quiet. One eye idly followed the squirrel's journey of exploration among the bags hanging from the ridge pole. His mind was a conflict of emotions. No second sight was needed to recognize the objects of the Indian's search. He could almost hear Red Whiskers and Hatchet Face bellowing about the two squaws and boy they had killed, while the wounded buck escaped. Before his eyes flashed the bloody wad of brown skin flaunted as a future tobacco pouch. Baffled anger clogged his throat. He felt his face pinch down into a savage scowl. It would need but a few words from him to send vengeance directly toward its rightful prey. On the other hand, how could he betray one of his own race to a half-naked heathen? Or contribute to possible deaths from the hands of such people as had dealt himself so much grief? His eyes lifted to the Calapooya's bow and arrow quiver hanging on the wall beside the knife belt. Surely it was right to see justice done, for redmen as well as white. But what right had he to lend his aid as judge and jury? It was a confusing problem! Long he sat before the dying coals, while the primitive side of his mind battled for expression against the more sober teachings of white generations.

"It'd be a losin' game for the Injun, anyhow, was I to set him onto that pair," he reasoned at last, his thoughts reaching for a justifiable conclusion. "If they didn't gun him down 'fore he got goin', the whole camp'd be after him like a hound pack. Some of 'em would be sure to git him e'er he got outa the valley. It'd be just like puttin' a rope 'round his neck. Nope, best let 'er lay. He's too good a meat for white butchers. And Pa allus held that no two sorry wrongs ne'er made one doubtful right."

He talked it over with Tenny the following morning. Drawn outside for a quick consultation, she readily agreed with him.

"There has been too much bloodshed already," she said bleakly. "And, as you say, telling him about those prospectors would lead him into nothing but danger. He has had enough trouble. It's to be hoped that time will somewhat cure his grief, as it seems to be curing ours."

Rance patted her shoulder and reached for the milk bucket. "Good girl! I reckoned as how you'd sight the thing in its best light. It might be we could even condition him to the notion that his medicine spilled him off the dam on purpose, just to halt him packin' the feud any longer."

"A splendid thought!" She flashed one of her starry-eyed smiles. "And it might just work. You do have the most marvelous ideas!"

He felt the warmth of her words climb high in his cheeks as he hurried off toward the barn. "Oh! Susanna" floated above his head. Mayhaps fate would decide the thing in due time, if let free to work without anybody's guesswork meddling in.

As if by mutual consent, neither of them mentioned the subject again. His story told, Joe likewise made no further allusion to his plans for revenge. He seemed content to stretch out on a blanket before the fire while his wounds healed and his body regained its vigor. His face showed only appreciation for the day's favors as he watched the others go about their work. Tenny voted him an ideal patient.

Rance complained good-naturedly that it made him feel like some old graybeard, the way his lightest suggestion was received by the Indian as though coming from the Great Spirit in person. As for Tenny, his grave black eyes followed her every move with wordless doglike devotion. In turn, the unfeigned interest that both of them showed in the Indian's descriptions of native customs and beliefs among the Calapooyas soon loosened all their tongues in a mutually enjoyable camaraderie. They got on famously.

"It looks as though we might have adopted us a boy," she told Rance one morning, looking up from her churning. "Or maybe we are the adopted ones. At any rate, he acts as though we all belonged together."

Rance nodded, pulling thoughtfully at his forelock. "It could be that he's sorta hitched hisself onto us for scarceness of any other folks. I misdoubt it'll carry on, though, once he gits up an' around. Injuns are said to be uncommon notional."

"Perhaps so. Yet he seemed to take it sensibly enough, when I explained how he would have to stay here and take care of things when we—you went to Jacksonville to sell your furs and keg of butter." She paused to scoop the remaining blobs of butter out of the churn, her hand revolving the wooden ladle with effortless dexterity, "And by the way," she added, "that keg of butter will only hold a couple more churnings."

"Uh-huh!" He twisted at his forelock, his sky-blue eyes staring blankly out the window. That break in her words about going to Jacksonville spawned an unsettling thought. "Gotta git that butter to the store 'fore the weather hottens up," he said, sparring for time to think. "The brine coverin' won't keep it everlastin'. Furs, too, should go. And—and I don't reckon you was mayhaps figgerin' to go along, was you?"

"I—I hadn't thought much about it." The hesitation in his voice tightened her throat. "It would be nice to see the stores and everything. But," a thin little sigh escaped her lips, "I—I'd likely feel pretty awkward, going out among town folks in my buckskins and moccasins."

"Wel-ll, 'tain't purely that." A vision of Ma's patched dress flashed before his mind. "I reckon's how some of the new settlers ain't over-tidy; not really liken town folks. But—but—well, my main misdoubt is leavin' Joe here alone to tend the stock an milkin'. Injun-like, he might take off anywheres, once we got gone."

"I see!" Tenny's back turned stiffly, hiding the eyes fastened on the last lump of fresh butter under her hands. Still keeping her face averted, she drained the last of the buttermilk out of the wooden trough and laid the scoop-shaped ladle aside. "I suppose there's no telling what he might do if one of us wasn't here to supervise things." She wiped a forearm across her eyes, turning back to face him. "Yes, it would certainly be better if I stayed here. Much better! Perhaps you would—could bring me a piece of new dress goods, along with some shoes and stockings. Then I wouldn't shame you completely, if we happened to meet anybody." She picked up the butter abruptly and disappeared into the springhouse.

CHAPTER 16

Rance, left alone, stood studying his feet. He felt like a mule-kicked hound-dog. Tenny remained out of sight in the springhouse.

Minutes later, he wandered aimlessly out to the barn, hands sunk deep in his pockets. A sour lump had suddenly appeared in his stomach. Even a gourd-head could see that she had been hankering to go to Jacksonville with him. No telling how long she had been favoring the idea, unbeknownst to anybody. Now his piddling excuse to leave her at home had plumb washed out all the pleasureness she had been storing up for nobody knew how long. And now she had gone off by herself to hide her crying. He felt like crying himself.

He hooked the barn door shut behind him and dropped face down on the straw-littered floor. Why hadn't he taken her to town when the snow first went off? Or while the snow was still on, for that matter? Every delay made it that much worse. Now he was up against a post. There was no question what folks would think, and say, at this late date, once they found out the two of them had been here alone all winter. They would simply crucify her! Him, too, probably. And it was all his fault. He just hadn't been man enough to face the lonesomeness of the cabin without her company. So he had dallied and piddled, easing himself from one broken-legged excuse to another, anything to put off the day when everybody must know the whole story. And she would be the main sufferer; women always got the heft of the blame. He beat his fists on the floor in a frenzy of bafflement. Jacksonville was a small place, but no place was too small to have its scandalmongers. Damn all the nosy old—! No, damn Rance Hardig for giving them the chance to shame Tenny! It made a body feel like loading up the wagon and taking her clean out of the country.

Yet there must be some way out of the difficulty. Pa always claimed brains were made for figuring hard problems: all a body had to do was yoke them to the right plow. Meanwhile, mighty nigh all he could see to do was put off the town trip for a stretch of time, while he studied on it.

The trouble was, unfortunately, that the more he studied the situation, the more confusing it became. Everything seemed to work against him. His original intention of taking her into Jacksonville immediately after the rescue would have cleared the whole thing up, without any bother. Almost any of the townspeople would have taken her in, once they had heard how he found her. But how was he to get her to town when she was sickened nigh onto death before daybreak? It was just as bad while she was making back to health. Only a witless gawk would have hauled her out in the cold, raddled as she was from the lung fever weakness. And even with her strength back to normal-like, she was still in no shape for a day's ride through snow up to a horse's shoulder. True, the Chinook and big thaw wiped out the weather problem, as time had wiped out the sickness hangover. She really could have gone then. But, honesty rose up to remind him, the thought of gossiping tongues had just plain held him off from doing anything about it. Or, and honesty again raised its head, mayhaps he simply didn't want her to go. Her cheerful company had been such a prideful gift. In the face of winter's long isolation ahead, and the dragging weeks of stark loneliness a haunting memory, life would have been right down sorrowful without her. An uneasy sense of guilt nagged at this excuse for unrightful selfishness. However, he had not really meant to wrong her. It was just—just—.

Anyway, before he could figure out a workable way to straighten things out, that arrow wound had headed off any immediate decision. He was forced to admit that it was something of a relief to have the troublesome problem shoved out of sight under his own difficulties, but mayhaps it was sort of a rightful thing, at that. What if he had got all fussed up and let her go before those scalphunters jumped him down by the creek? It stood to reason he would not have been doing himself any favor by having rushed her off sometime earlier. This last deal with the Calapooya was about the same: without her hankering for a springtime walk, they would never have gone up to the dam or found the boy in time to save his life. Also, and he pulled ruefully at his forelock, it was Tenny's quick thinking that had saved him from murdering the defenseless Indian in cold blood. Come to figure it all up, it looked mighty like nothing would have panned out right, had he got rid of the girl on the start. The whole thing sort of piled up like the Bible book said about God directing a body's footsteps, when the fellow wasn't nowise able to see right sure where he was going.

"It shore snarls a body's thinkin'," he told himself dispiritedly. "Doin' what I ought butts head-on inta doin' what I did, while doin' what I want gits tromped underfoot by both of 'em. Round an' round, like a dog a-chasin' its tail! It's enough to set a body pickin' at the bedclo'es. And now Tenny's all broke up over me not seein' fit to let her go where folks'll make shame of things she reckons naught of. Mappin' out the deal to her would likely make her feel worse an' hate me more'n ever, prob'ly just for me a-thinkin' such unrightful thoughts; and not explainin'd leave both of us kickin' shins in the dark. It shore looks like the Devil's come for his dues, an' me with no pitch hot."

Nor did the following days offer any solution to the problem. Rance explored every visible avenue of thought, only to find bafflement shunting him back into the same dreary waste from whence he had started. Gloom rode his shoulders in the daytime and grinned mockingly at him from above the fireplace during the evenings. Tenny retired within herself, after her few weak attempts at cheerfulness met only gruff responses. Her eyes stared expressionlessly at the far corner of the room for seemingly endless moments; her firmly set lips no longer brought laugh wrinkles crinkling up beside her nose. The feeling of being rejected fanned Rance's unreasoned resentment. He kept his eyes stubbornly on his plate when at the table, and left the room as soon as possible after the meal was over.

"Let 'er chaw on 'er own rind. She craves to shun my comp'ny, it's nothing' to me!" He kicked savagely at a rock in his path. The bruised toe did nothing to brighten his feelings. "'S what a feller gits for tryin' to figger ways of savin' her more grief—soon's I kin."

Tenny stood back from the open door, watching him go. Her lips closed in a thin line. She dabbed at her eyes with the edge of the dishcloth. The stubborn self-centered fool! She bit down hard on the thought. Wants to shut me out of everything but work. Ashamed to be seen with me among the town folks. Afraid to even speak decent for fear she'd take advantage of it. Well, he needn't worry! She knew how to keep her mouth shut. Tight! And she'd certainly never ask to go anywhere with him again. The nearest to that would be to maybe trail him out to the settlement, where she could take off on her own and never see him again. She ran into the bedroom to fling herself face down on the bed.

"The hateful brute!" she sobbed brokenly against the pillow.

The Indian didn't know what to make of his friends' actions. There had been no open quarrel or loud voices. Rance had made no threatening motions with a stick, as was often necessary to keep peace in one's lodge. The girl went through each night without any attempt to cut off her man's hair in his sleep, or burn his moccasins. Instead, both of them seemed mainly interested in avoiding each other as much as possible, after exchanging only dark looks in place of open speech. It was very puzzling. Surely there must be some evil thing in Yellow Hair's lodge to cause so much darkness in both minds.

Meanwhile, he kept much to himself, his expressionless eyes ever watchful for some lessening of the tension between the two. With the healing of his wounds, he spent the bulk of his time in the woods. The deer were still poor, after their long winter in the deep snow, but his snares yielded many rabbits and grouse for the table. Once he was gone for two days. Rance suspected him of scouting the trails toward the settlement, hoping for a sight of the white killers. He said nothing, however, when the Indian returned one evening as silently as he had gone. Rance threw out several hints as to where he might have been, but his efforts availed nothing. The Indian's evasiveness was somewhat covered by an odd block of wood he had found someplace, and to which he now turned all his attention in the guise of busy whittling, whenever any mention was made of his private affairs. Left to himself, he would often spend his time silently watching the others at their work or disappear into the timber for long hours at a stretch. One afternoon, he displayed an unusual interest in watching Rance bale his furs in a press he had devised by attaching a pole lever to the barn wall.

"You Yellow Hair mak' good fur pack," he grunted. "Mos' lak' McKenzie River trapper, but more better push-together."

Rance grinned his acknowledgment of the praise, inviting the Indian to manage the press while he bound the pile of skins with strings of tough cedar bark. Joe was glad to comply. This was something that really interested him. They had a pleasant afternoon, made more so to Rance by the simplification of the task under the other's willingness to help.

"You tak' to trader pos' pretty quick now, eh?" Joe asked, as they finished piling the bales in the shed.

"Oh, someday. Don't know just when."

"White miss go 'long for trade, too?"

"Well-l," Rance's fingers strayed to his forelock. "I dunno as she will. She seems kinda soured on my comp'ny right now."

"That why she no talk?"

"Reckon so. Gone crossgrain somehow."

"You have bad thoughts, mebbyso?"

"She'd give anybody bad thoughts, havin' to sulk about things she don't know the why of." A sullen harshness had crept suddenly into his voice.

"Bad spirit mebbyso mak' sulk for both. Find good spirit, ever'body feel fine. Then have big fun, lak' other times."

"You don't understand anything about it. I ain't to blame." Rance kicked a bale of furs back into the corner. "I'm doin' the best I kin. If she hones to spite me, just outa orneriness, I guess I've got a right to spite back."

Joe walked off, shaking his head. His friend, Yellow Hair, better find good medicine pretty quick, or bad spirits make his head go "ding-ding!" like mission house bell.

CHAPTER 17

Rance's talk with the Indian did nothing to make him feel better. By morning, he was downright miserable. Things hadn't looked so hopeless since Pa and Ma were first taken. He worked half-heartedly at repairing the wooden harrow, made from half a dozen lateral poles bored for the tough oak pegs that helped pulverize the earth. It was a caution how many of the pegs got broken in just one season. Hang-tight roots, still lurking treacherously beneath the newly cleared field would, it seemed, tear anything to pieces. He shaped the ninth replacement with his hatchet, then found seven more with deceitful cracks, evidently trying to cozen him into false trust until they could let go in the middle of some busy forenoon. He drove a peg into place with spiteful blows of his hatchet. Everything seemed bent on laying back to gouge him when he wasn't looking.

Nor did changing jobs help. When he went down in the bottom to cut poles for an extension of the meadow pasture fence shortly after dinner, the whole area was apparently in league to cause his downfall. As he was crossing the creek, a rock turned under his foot, soaking him to the crotch before he could scramble to dry land. Later, a wild swing of his axe caught an unnoticed tree branch, twisting the implement out of his hand and all but slicing into his foot. A falling tree kicked back at him, as it left the stump. He barely escaped, throwing himself into a clump of wild gooseberries that left him picking out thorns for half an hour. A blue jay laughed raucously at his discomfiture. The old owl hooted its mournful lament between its hollow thumpings on the dead snag. Rance was glad to see the sun go down, even though the twilight threw spectral shadows in his path all the way to the cabin.

Even Tenny's tasty supper did nothing to brighten his mood. His spirits drooped still lower as occasional sidelong glances saw her clear away the supper things, her hard, dry eyes as uncompromising as the thin line of her lips.

Joe had withdrawn into a world of his own, even more removed than his usual soberness. He spent most of his time hunched over in a far corner, silently carving on his block of wood. Even the shifting firelight and wavering candle flames seemed to have joined in the conspiracy of hostile, brooding silence.

Rance felt like he had been marooned on a dreary island lost in a dark sea of loneliness. When he could stand it no longer, he got to his feet and went outside. Bitterness fogged his mind as he stared into the darkness, a darkness no blacker than his milling thoughts.

"And after all I've tried to favor her, too!" he muttered under his breath. "Acts like I was fixin' to cut her throat for pure spite. And now she's got Joe a-settin' against me, too. Anything to pile up the miserables! I've a prime notion to pull out some'eres, whilst waitin' for seedin' time. I shore, Lord, ain't wanted 'round here."

It was long after he heard the bedroom door slam shut that he went back into the cabin.

But where would he go, if he did leave? The question kept sleep at bay for what seemed an interminable time. All he could think of was the spring trip to Jacksonville. That, however, would only add fuel to the fire, as things now stood. Anyway, the thought of Jacksonville had suddenly become more repulsive than attractive. It was kind of like the feel of entering a haunted house or walking over dead bodies. He couldn't understand it.

The morning sun, fortunately, washed the worst of his dejection away. It was a lovely day. The squirrel chittered merrily at him from its perch on the ridgepole of the cabin. The owl's drumming had a livelier note. Scent of growing things floated around his head on the soft morning air. He fingered thoughtfully at his forelock as he went out to the barn shortly after breakfast.

Halfway to the barn, a roving thought suddenly sprang out of nowhere to clamor for attention. His feet slowed to a dragging halt.

"Good a time as any," he told himself. "I've been fixin' to git the buryin' of her folks' remains tended to right soon, anyhow, now't the snow's gone. It might soften up her unreasonin' a mite, was I to go do it now. And it would be right down peaceful up there all day by myself."

His legs picked up their stride automatically. Yes, that would take him out of the troubled atmosphere for the time being, at least. And off by himself, he might be able to figure out something for Tenny, short of running her into a plumb deadfall.

He caught the gray mare in the corral before she could make her usual escape to the pasture. That was a good sign. Joe would undoubtedly see it as something to do with his medicine out-fading the evil spirits that had been dogging his trail the past two days. Well, mayhaps he would have the right of it. It was hard to tell about spirits, the way things had been running lately.

His eyes ran around the clearing for sight of the Indian. There was nothing to be seen of him. Mayhaps that was just as well. He didn't need any company today, even if it was somebody able to picture him being blessed by a bunch of heathen spirits. He grinned crookedly as he cinched his saddle on the gray mare and tied the worn-bladed spade under the stirrup leather.

Of Tenny there was no sign. She had made no appearance outside the cabin since breakfast. Nor was she in evidence when he went in to get his rifle. He thought he heard the bedroom door close just as he came up on the doorstep, but he couldn't be sure. However, it didn't matter. He wasn't aiming to tell her where he was going, nohow. She wouldn't loosen up enough to appreciate it, doggonit! He jerked the gray mare around with unfeeling roughness as he climbed into the saddle. Mayhaps he would just keep on going. He might as well, and pleasure everybody. He jammed the leather hat down over his eyes. Moments later, he was headed up the creek, without a backward glance, to disappear into the timber.

It was an hour later when Joe made his soundless appearance, drifting around the end of the cabin from out of nowhere. He hunkered down beside the doorway to resume his interminable carving. One eye fastened itself on Tenny, now busy with an armful of dirty clothes beside the big wash kettle. There weren't many clothes, her own underwear and the shift she wore under the buckskin dress, Pa's old pants that Rance used for a change, two pairs of socks, assorted flour, sugar, and salt sacks that served for handkerchiefs and dishcloths, and the old canvas patched pants they had given the Indian; but it was a duty not to be neglected.

The Indian's covert glance searched her face for long moments as she worked, bent over the washboard Pa had made by corrugating the face of a tamarack slab. A veil of thought settled over his eyes.

"Li'l white miss mebbyso t'row cloud on heart of Yellow

Hair?" he said softly, as though speaking to himself. He paused, studying his carving for a moment. Then: "Li'l cloud mak' big cloud, big cloud mak' bad storm; all t'row down tree an' mak' good lodge go 'Poof!'"

Tenny looked up, her face stormy. "It's not my doing. He shuns me for no real cause. And I—I tried—"

Her voice choked off in a sob as she turned back to her washing. The way she slammed the big wooden lid on the kettle brought the Indian to his feet with a jerk. He tucked his carving under one arm.

"One cloud let sun t'rough, other clouds go 'way," he said with the same softness, reaching for his bow and quiver. "White miss hol' sun in hands," he added over his shoulder.

When she looked up to reply, the Indian had disappeared. She scoured at her eyes with a reddened hand. The sound of her mumbled words was drowned in the lonesome braying of the Buck mule. One side of her mind hoped Rance would keep going wherever he was headed for. And never come back! The other part followed his trail up the creek, speculating on his return, and how soon. He couldn't be going far, surely, leaving that fence half-finished, and it such a lovely day for work. Or could be? The way he had been drooping around, a person would think his wits had gone on a vacation for sure. Well, she didn't care one whit! Let him act like an addled goose, if he wanted to. Who cared? Her brow puckered thoughtfully. It was mighty odd, though, that he had never mentioned any call to desert his work for a horseback ride.

Rance, for his part, felt the soggy blanket of depression gradually melt away under the warmth of budding spring. The sense of well-being climbed higher in his thoughts with each bend of the creek. He found his ears lifting eagerly to the amorous drumming of a grouse, somewhere up on the hillside. A great wedge of northbound geese honked their cheerful way overhead. The creek sang its thanks for the rich perfume showered down so freely by bursting buds. The whole world smelled sweeter, the farther he went. "Oh! Susanna" hung on his lips as Tenny walked into his thoughts. He caught himself halfway wishing he had asked her to come with him. This was the kind of a ride she would purely enjoy, even on the back of the Buck mule.

He scowled the vision away, his body jerking stiffly upright. One hand clenched itself around the saddle horn, it's knuckles standing out white against the tanned skin.

"She wouldn'ta come, anyhow," he growled through tightened lips. "Not with her bile a-runnin' over, liken it is. 'Sides, this job'll be nothing upliftin' for her to see; mostly bones by now. Mayhaps later in the summer, agin I git things cleared up an' it grows over. She mi—"

A latent memory of his neglect to plan something definite about her future rose up to push the rest of his sentence down his throat. Later in the summer suddenly took shape as a bare and dreary waste—with Tenny gone.

He turned slowly up the hill away from the creek, all the seductive sweetness drained from the air. His mind was revolving in jerky circles, like a driftlog in a whirlpool. Tenny gone? No! He sucked in his breath, trying to fill a vast empty spot. He couldn't stand that! But suppose nothing like that happened? It could be that some scrannelly bedevilment had witched his thinking plumb out of line. The Jacksonville folks would likely be powerful busy at this time of year; they probably wouldn't pay a bit of mind to strangers dropping in. And to cinch things up tighter against any chancy prying, it would be no trick for her to rig herself up to look like a boy. She'd make a right down handsome boy! Then mayhaps they could go right on living that way, without anybody sensing the difference. Why hadn't he thought of that before?

The world of Rance Hardig brightened up for all of five minutes. Then doubt again raised its ugly head in a mocking grin. He must be off his wits entirely. Any gilly might know that such a scheme would never work with Tenny. She had no inkling of poison tongues hungering for fodder, or what they might do to her, allowed half a chance. And trying to explain things would like as not snarl her thoughts up with the feel that he was charging her with wrongdoing. Any auguring that she fault herself by wearing man's clothes would be just as bad. Any way you looked at it, such misbegotten notions would purely upset her to where she might take off in the first handy direction, like a shot-stung deer.

He thumped his heels spitefully against the gray mare's ribs, only to receive a baleful sidewise glance in return. The mare was scrambling up a scab-rock slope, and didn't appreciate being told how to go about it. Rance slumped back in the saddle. The old mare's stubbornness was just like everything else, a thing to spite him. His head sagged like a dried-out camas bloom. His thoughts took up the same old weary circle.

"If I'd done it first off—But 'twasn't nowise possible then—and later, that old killin' lonesomeness was starin' me in the face." His muffled voice droned on. "What was a body to do?"

CHAPTER 18

The mare topped out on the hill and livened her pace up the ridge. Rance lifted his chin out of his chest to make sure of his bearings. His eyes were bleak as a stranded catfish. Yonder, the saddle-shaped peak shadowed the little flat where he had found Tenny.

"Poor little Tenny!" Her tear-streaked face swam into his vision. "She was so needful of somebody that day. And she still is. I can't let her run herself into a deadfall."

Still, how could he help it? He squirmed uneasily, tugging at his forelock. Some things just naturally slipped up on a body's blind side to stop him cold. The odds were all stacked against both of them. It seemed like when two people had nothing but each other, the good Lord might lend a hand at fixing up some kind of a deal that would keep them together.

Together? Together! He sat up straighter, his mind racing. Like a family was together? His eyes flared wide. Why, that was it! That would fix everything. Just like Pa and Ma! Tenny was the whole answer. That would put her in the clear, wash out the threat of hurtful tongues, and cure forever all this lonesomeness for both of them, all at one swipe. Why, it was simple as two and two. Or rather, he grinned to himself, one and one. He wondered how he could have overpassed such a simple thing all this while. He must have been as witless as a pole-axed steer.

The awed gaze of a discoverer facing a new world swung in a slow and somewhat dizzy half circle. A noonday sun spilled its shining light down the side of the saddle peak, cleaving a path through the scattered timber. It caught Rance's glance, pulling his eyes upward to the great bowl of fathomless blue sky. An almost stifling warmth rose in his chest. Something without sound or substance hung in the breathless air.

"Dear God!" he whispered. "You did open the gate in a right down handsome way. I'm shore most purely grateful for showin' me the entryway inta this new pasture. Mayhaps I'll be able to kinda square things a mite by makin' Tenny extra happy. I hope so. I'm shore a-fixin' to do my best."

He thumped the gray into motion and rode on.

The wonder of his discovery, however, stayed with him. He didn't expect to catch God looking down at him from the top of Saddle Peak, but he must be hovering around somewhere mighty close. That answer to his off-hand call for help had been too prompt to travel any great long stretch.

And Tenny? Of course, he would have to hear her say on the matter. Marrying was said to be a somewhat ponderable thing for a girl. But he was tolerably sure she held a right smart leaning toward the same idea, or would as soon as she found out his true feelings.

He closed his eyes momentarily, giving over to the flood of enchantment that suddenly enveloped him. To have Tenny with him the whole time of their lives; to love her whenever he was so notioned; to have the wedded right of kissing that soft curve of her neck, where the tiny little curls lay like rose petals against the white skin. The sheer joy of anticipation ran through his veins in a hot flood. His heart thudded against his ribs at the thought of sharing the big bedroom with her; of planning their future together; of going swimming in the big beaver pond on moonlit nights; of sharing secrets and everyday problems that were theirs alone. He felt ten feet tall and strong as a he-grizzly bear.

Even the sobering sight of the burnt wagon was not enough to entirely subdue his spirits. Eyes dazzled by the glow of tomorrow's promise have little sight for fading yesterdays. And acute reminders of the tragedy had been softened by time and weather. Weight of the heavy winter snow had crushed the fire-weakened wagon body to the ground. Storm and wind had scoured its surface to a dirty dark gray. Both hind wheels leaned drunkenly toward each other, held in place only by the charred axle ends sunk in the wet ground. Coyotes, buzzards, and magpies had scattered the contents of the flattened wagon box in all directions. There was little left to suggest any immediate connection with flesh-and-blood humans.

Rance swung down from the saddle, his eyes registering what needed to be done. He untied the spade from beneath the stirrup leather to stand for a moment, leaning on its handle. The gray mare, reins dragging, drifted out across the flat toward a scattering of green shoots thrusting themselves above the winterflattened grass.

He turned to start gathering what bones he could find. "It makes a right piddlin' sight for a buryin'," he reflected, "but there seems naught I can do about that. At least I won't have to put Tenny in mind of how slight it was. She'll be happy to know they're taken care of proper-like, 'thout any needin' to tally details."

Digging was easy in the soft ground, still spongy from melting snows. It was a short task to make the narrow hole deep enough for safety against burrowing animals. Rance mumbled what he could remember of the Lord's Prayer as, sprawled on the grass with head and arms down in the hole, he arranged the bones in neat order. Reverently he laid the charred boot, now badly chewed by unknown scavengers, on top of the little heap, all the while trying to shut his ears against the sound of dismembered foot bones rattling against the inside of the warped leather. Moments later, he hurriedly replaced the freshly dug earth, tramping it solid under his feet. He rounded the mound up neatly, after placing a large triangular rock upright in the hole.

"That'll stand to mark the spot aginst time an' weather," he assured himself. "I'll make out to gouge their names on it later on, should Tenny take a liken to the idea."

He walked back to what had once been a wagon. There he began scraping the debris away with his spade. A few scraps of metal rattled under his feet. An iron cooking pot lay in two pieces, a victim of heated metal deluged with snow. The metal parts of a worn plow stared bleakly at him from its resting place between the two hind wheels. A rusted tin box yielded a single bone china plate and two cups, all that was left intact among a jumble of broken pieces. Rance laid the three undamaged pieces aside. Tenny would probably cherish things like that, for keepsakes. Then, in dumping out the broken scraps, his eye lighted on a woman's small brooch among the litter. It was a delicate piece of porcelain set in burnished silver. He rubbed the accumulated dirt from its face before pinning it inside his shirt pocket.

"Tenny's gift from her ma." He twisted his forelock sharply as something rose hard in his throat. "And just to think it stayed here for the findin' this whole time! It's a wonder thing that nigh shakes believin'."

He stared up at the peak, hoping God still had an eye out for the kind of thankfulness that hauled a body's heart plumb up through his windpipe.

Riding homeward, the dishes tucked safely inside his shirt, his mind took another turn of dodging between hopefulness and despair. A tardy memory of Tenny's recent hostility rose up to tear his fine plans into shreds. Was she really as angry as she had seemed? Would he be able to soften her disposition with his love talk? Had his balking about the Jacksonville trip soured her for good, or was it just a passing thing? Mayhaps these gifts from the dead would help knock that chip off of her shoulder. At least, he hoped they wouldn't call back the old grief enough to set her off in some worse kind of withholding herself. The latter possibility stopped the breath in his throat for a moment. That would mean she had no true heart love for him. Real heart love didn't let itself be plowed under by little misdoubts. No, it couldn't be like that, not the way he was feeling. Mayhaps his caring for her family's remains would sway her in his direction, but that seemed like a mighty trifling foundation for building a dream on. Telling her right out about how much she meant to him, and how it had suddenly roused him to their future need for each other might help. He felt the words slowly shaping themselves on his lips. But what if she stiffened up, like she had been doing, and refused to listen? He groaned inwardly.

"I shore wish Ma had taught me something about what to expect from woman thinkin'," he said plaintively, thumping the gray mare to a faster gait.

The bright side of his mind was still trying to keep its ragged fringes out of the mire of dejection as he at last trotted the gray mare out into the home clearing shortly after sundown. His eyes ran quickly around the place. What seemed like a strange quiet hung heavy in the air. No noise of hands, busy with supper preparations, came from the cabin. The door stood half-open, swaying gently on its pin hinges. No smoke drifted above the stone chimney. Old Brockle bawled inquiringly from the corral.

But it was the slim poles Tenny had persuaded him to fashion for a clothes-drying rack that at last caught and held his sweeping glance. Most of her morning's washing still dangled from the poles. Why, his mind inquired, had she left the clothes out until almost dark, when it had been such a fine drying day? Then, on the heels of the question, his gaze stopped short on the willow clothes basket. It lay on its side, its contents scattered as though dragged about and trampled into the dirt. Naked fear started climbing his backbone, digging icy toenails into his body at every step. Something had happened while she was gathering the clothes!

Silently cursing himself for having been gone all day, he tumbled out of the saddle and raced for the cabin. What had happened? Was Tenny hurt? Had that cussed Indian—?

He stumbled through the door, almost falling over the washboard. He caught his balance, eyes wide with dread sweeping the room. Nothing amiss there, except the uncleared breakfast table. He plunged into the bedroom. Only the unmade bed met his searching gaze. The leanto was equally deserted. He circled the scantily furnished rooms again. Nothing! One hand pulled at his forelock. Only one fact stood out: the girl had gone outside to hang up the clothes, shortly after he left. Then the ominous something, whatever it was, had taken place before she could return to attend the housework. But what?

Stark terror twisted his face. Why hadn't he taken her with him? Of all the stubborn fools! He rushed outside, knocking his hat off against the door frame and spinning himself half around. Still staggering from the collision, he ran back to the clothes-rack. There should be some helpful sign left there. But nothing definite showed itself. Scuff marks and the overturned basket told of some sort of a struggle. Various garments had plainly been walked on or kicked aside, but the whole scene was too confused for any clear understanding.

Bafflement pulled his face into a strained mask. He straightened up, both fists clenched, as black rage swept over him. There might be some clue down in the creek bottom or on the trail. There had to be.

He swung half around. "That damned Injun! I was scared he—"

CHAPTER 19

It was midway of his turn that one eye caught a suggestion of movement. He leaned forward tensely. Someone was coming out of the timber twilight, a hundred yards up the creek trail from the cabin. He dashed a hand across his eyes. The shadowy figure moved slowly out into the open. Yes, it was Tenny! Now he could see her clearly. It was easy to make out the disheveled hair stringing in wisps around her dirt-smeared face. The buckskin blouse was awry, too, its lacings ripped loose to expose half her chest. And what looked like a bloody scratch ran all the way down one shin from the edge of her skirt. She walked as though in a trance, stony-eyed and grim-lipped. And not far behind her stalked the Indian.

"Tenny!" Rance's broken cry rang across the clearing. He was lunging toward her with great loping strides. "Oh, Tenny! Where you been? What happened?"

She came on, moving woodenly, without saying anything.

Even when he reached her, arms outspread and breath rasping hoarsely, she brushed by him without a word. He stopped in astonishment, one arm still extended in her direction. His lips fumbled for words. Then, before he could speak further, she suddenly broke into a run and fled toward the cabin.

He stood rooted to the ground, his mouth half open. Surprise, puzzlement, anger, and despair fought for command of his emotions. Like a wounded animal, he slowly followed her.

The pursuit, however, was fruitless. By the time he reached the cabin, she had disappeared into the bedroom. The cabin seemed more desolate than ever.

"Tenny!" he called, rapping on the bedroom door. "Hey, Tenny, let me talk to you!" He tried the latch, then put his weight forcibly against the door. Its slight movement, before halting with definite immobility, told him the inside bar had been dropped against his entrance. The rough planks seemed to stare back at him in sullen defiance. "Tenny, I just gotta see you! Please!"

The only answer was a muffled "Go away! Leave me alone!" He couldn't tell whether her voice was coming through tears or anger.

Further pounding on the door and calling her name brought no results whatever. Baffled frustration finally turned him away in despair. His dragging feet carried him blindly across the room. One hand unconsciously drifted to the uncomfortable weight pulling down on his bloused shirt. He felt, without seeing, the hand remove the three pieces of china and set them on the fireplace mantel. With like absentness, he unpinned the porcelain brooch to lay it in one of the cups. Gone was all the joy of returning the keepsake treasures. Let her find them in her own good time, to use as she saw fit. It didn't matter. Nothing mattered!

It was the low voice of the Indian that brought him to the door. Joe was squatted against the wall, his bow across his knees. Rance paused beside him, a flood of questions crowding against his lips.

"What happened?" he asked, sorting his words. "You tell—all!" His voice was harshly threatening in its intensity.

"Joe see all bad t'ing. Joe tell Yellow Hair friend. Mak'

Yellow Hair glad me save white miss from *cultus* white mans who kill Calapooya women."

Rance dropped to his knees, one hand seizing the Indian's arm in a viselike grip. "Wha—what do you mean? What about women killers?"

"Joe tell of bad white mans kill brother's wives an' son, one tam." He shoved Rance's hand aside with a half smile. "Brother speak good picture of w'at killers look lak'. Joe come for hunt these mans. Me tell; you know 'bout dat." It was a flat statement.

Rance knew. He had readily recognized the Indian's description of Red Whiskers and the fishy-eyed Hatchet Face. And, more than he had ever dared openly admit to himself, blindly concealed the fact out of deference to his own race. Now the whole thing had backfired to explode in his own face. He chewed at his lip.

"Yes, I do remember what you tell," he said at last. "Now you tell of this bad thing today!"

The Indian nodded, launching himself immediately into his account of the day's happenings.

He had, he said, seen Rance ride away with his heart on the ground. Such persons do not like company. Joe, accordingly, went off by himself to avoid intrusion. His snares were soon inspected, leaving him the rest of the day to be idled away until the other's return.

It was still early. He was seated up on the hill, perhaps half a mile from the cabin, when he spied two mounted men leading a packhorse up the creek trail toward the cabin. About that time, Tenny came out in the yard to hang up her wet clothes. She evidently caught the eyes of the men, for they stopped to watch her from behind a heavy brush clump. A short consultation and some moments of scanning the place closely apparently satisfied them that she was alone. The pair then quickly led their horses up behind the barn, carefully keeping the building between themselves and the girl. There, they tied the animals before walking casually on to the cabin. Tenny was caught by surprise. They were between her and the cabin before she realized their presence. They, however, acted friendly, making some kind of conversation until they were almost upon her.

Rance could see it all. Quite likely, she had considered them to be merely friendly neighbors. In her innocence, she might have even mentioned her connection with Rance as the only survivors of the two families. She might also have told them about his having gone off in the hills for the day. All that could have easily opened the door to what followed.

What followed was the bodily seizure of the girl by the two ruffians. Joe had been unable to make out many details from his distant viewpoint, while scattered timber and brush hid most of her final struggle. His race back to the cabin netted him only the sight of her being lashed bodily onto the back of the loaded packhorse. By the time he reached the clearing, the abductors had crossed the creek to head southeast into the hills, well away from the trail. He was still panting from his long run as he saw them disappear into the timber on the opposite side of the meadow. Fortunately, he had gained enough distance that he was able to recognize the described murderers of his brother's family. Nobody could mistake that surly face framed by bristly red whiskers and the man whose dead-fish eyes seemed to be hung straddle of a tomahawk blade.

The sight of those two would have been all he actually needed to set him in dogged pursuit. Now, as well, he had his yellow-haired brother's woman to save from the fate his own people had suffered. This double burden of retribution set him on the prospectors' trail with vengeance intensified.

His rather abashed excuse for being so long in overtaking them, was his winded condition at the start and the swifter speed of mounted men during the chase. As it was, the sun was past its full height before he caught up with them.

"Where'd you find 'em?" Rance's bared teeth shone wolfishly in the fading light.

The Indian swung his arm to the southeast. "'Way back. Cross t'ree crik'." Then he settled down to take up his story.

The two men had stopped for a midday camp in a pocket-like grassy meadow. Joe wormed his way up through a patch of huckleberry brush as they dismounted and turned the horses loose to graze. By the time Hatchet Face got a fire going and Red Whiskers finished untying their captive, the Indian was almost upon them. Bellied down under a bush, he saw Red Whiskers drag the girl to the ground and start tearing at her blouse.

"Did he abuse her person?" Rance hissed thickly.

"Tear clo'es an' pull hair to hol' down. Strike once in face. White miss fight lak' wil'cat. Then Fisheye come help hol'."

"And—and then?"

Joe held up a hand for silence. The rest had been easy, he said. Two carefully placed arrows had stopped the prospectors before they could reach their guns. His tomahawk had finished the affair a moment later. The death of his people had been avenged.

"And Tenny wasn't hurt bad, or truly wronged?" Rance broke in.

Joe shook his head. Fright and the rough handling had left her sick and weak, but not seriously damaged. Hearing the men discuss their plan to take her with them for the summer's prospecting, and Red Whisker's statement that "A cut throat'll stop any talkin' when it's time to go back for winterin' in the settlement," had perhaps been harder on her than the actual mistreatment. However, by the time he had dragged the two murderers into a nest of boulders and covered them with a pile of rocks, her tearful collapse had given way to a stony, white-faced silence. She managed to choke down some food under his forceful command, but flatly refused to ride either of the horses. He had to bring her home on foot. There was no other way. He spread his hands wide.

Rance dropped his arms around the other's shoulders. "Wonderous!" he breathed. "You done a truly prideful thing. Only a friend like you could save my heart from dying."

"Is good, my brother. White miss long sleep now. Feel good for Yellow Hair when morning come."

"I hope so!" Thought of Tenny's forbidding actions chilled the enthusiasm of Joe's words. Fresh uncertainty blurred his voice. "You really figure she's all right?"

"Plenty all right. No hurt. Jus' big scare mak' bad thought 'bout ever't'ing. Pretty quick be fine, lak' ol' tam'."

"I hope so, Joe," Rance said huskily. "I'll figger it that way for now. And do a scad of wishin'."

"Plenty good!" Joe got to his feet. "Me go now."

"Best not." Rance shrugged out of his own troubles to grasp the position his friend had put himself into on Tenny's behalf. "You stay here! Tenny an' me kin clear you, should anybody come a-quizzin'. We'll keep you sheltered long as you want. That'd be better'n runnin' off, where the first white man might kill you on sight."

Joe pondered a moment. Then: "No, me go. Work all done. Go Umpqua lodge easy, wit' t'ree horses an' plenty grub. No sun in lodge of my pipples till Joe come an' mak' glad hearts."

He started moving away, then suddenly turned to dash back into the cabin.

Rance didn't even bother to wonder what he had forgotten. His own thoughts were again milling through the fog that shrouded the closed bedroom door. Then the Indian was back, stepping up silently to lift Rance's hand against his own heart.

"Yellow Hair fine brother, always," he said softly. "My lodge be your lodge when sum'tam come. Bring white miss for big feast. Mak' all hearts glad."

Then he was gone, vanishing wraithlike into the early dark.

Rance turned aimlessly back into the cabin. Its emptiness mocked him silently. He glanced half-hopefully at the bedroom door. No, it had lost none of its forbidding grimness. There was no sound from within. His steps echoed hollowly as he crossed to the table and lighted the half-burned candle. Weary hands shoved the unwashed breakfast dishes aside. Sudden ravenous hunger led him to take down the trencher of cold meat from the shelf cupboard. He rummaged a handful of biscuits out of the breadbox. It had been a long day.

He started to sit down, then made another trip to the bedroom door. His rattling of the latch and pleas for some answer brought no more response than before. Morosely, he returned to the table. It was the most miserable meal he thought he had ever eaten.

The leanto was equally desolate. Joe's disordered blanket reminded him of some dead shell from which life had suddenly vanished. Even the pet squirrel had disappeared on business of its own. Tired as he was, he couldn't induce sleep to cross the void left by Tenny's withdrawal and the Indian's abrupt departure. The old, haunting loneliness of a soul bereft of all that made life worth living sogged over him like a wet blanket. It seemed like hours that he stared wide-eyed into the surrounding darkness. His mind caromed endlessly between the burial mission, his own empty future, the Indian's revenge, and Tenny's behavior. The last thing he remembered was the fragile hope that he would find her busy with breakfast preparations, her old cheerfulness again lighting the cabin, when he awoke.

But it was a wasted hope. He slept late. The sun was already high when he roused himself groggily to face the new day. Yesterday's heavy silence still hung like a pall over the cabin. He slipped into his clothes and, still barefooted, went into the other room. He stared around half-fearfully. It was like walking into a tomb. All the cold emptiness of the evening before rushed up to slap him in the face. No fire glowed in the fireplace, dirty dishes still cluttered the table, the air of hopeless abandonment hung over everything like a smothering black cloud. Then he saw the bedroom door standing half open.

He stood in his tracks for a long moment, not daring to hope, half fearing to breathe. Then, with a questioning cry, he rushed headlong for the door. Inside the room, he slid to a stop, almost falling across the bed. He looked around wildly. Light from the rawhide window was suffused in a warm glow. It picked up the outline of the chest of drawers bulking solidly against the north wall. He swung back to face the bed. He half choked on the stifled exclamation, as he took in the neatly spread quilts. Everything was in its rightful place. But there was no Tenny under the quilts. Tenny was definitely gone.

CHAPTER 20

But where had she gone? Not far, surely! Rance dashed out into the yard, eyes sweeping the clearing. Nothing stirred. Yesterday's washing still swayed lazily on the pole rack. The overturned basket hadn't been moved. His full-throated shouts brought no reply. A hurried circuit of the house and barn revealed nothing. The springhouse was empty. There was nothing to be seen of her down along the creek, while the roothouse door was securely fastened on the outside. There was no place else she could hide.

"I reckon as how she musta plumb lit out for some'eres," he concluded bleakly. "But where would she go, not knowin' anybody or anything about the country? And why spite me enough to go anywheres?" His voice ended in a hopeless note.

He shook his head gloomily and went back into the cabin. The bedroom held the same haunting spookiness that had followed Ma's death. It made him think of some unseen thing hovering back in the shadows under the rafters. He hurriedly reexamined the bed, chest of drawers, and the clothes-hanging corner. Her jacket no longer hung on its wall peg, and a quick search discovered that her cracked shoes were missing. That meant she figured on being gone for good. And what made it worse was that he could find no sign of any letter or note to tell what she had in mind. Not even a goodby! He shut the door behind him with the feeling of turning his back on a grave. Even the light from the new rawhide window seemed to have something funereal about it.

The main room wasn't much better. The cold fireplace, the uncleared table, the breathless silence, all seemed to point at him accusingly. Why hadn't he chanced taking her to Jacksonville, the way she wanted? It probably wouldn't have hurt anything. Why hadn't he asked her to go with him yesterday? Why hadn't he stayed at home, where he belonged, so he could have protected her? Why hadn't he tried to cheer her up, instead of going mule-stubborn on her?

"Plumb witless!" he accused himself. "Dumb as a blind hog in a cornfield. Faulted her to hide my own shame. Should have my hide peeled an' stretched over a hot fire!" But that wasn't any help now. He wished he could think of something that might right things. His head felt like it was stuffed with wet rags. It was hard to figure anything with a mind that just kept jumping in and out of the same dark hole. His wandering gaze fell on the coffeepot. "Mayhaps a slug of coffee'd help clear me up so'st I could study something halfway."

He was glad to find half a pot of the brew left from the day before. The blaze of pitch splinters brought a cloud of fragrant steam to his nostrils, awakening a surge of hunger. It was then, as he rummaged for food, that he noticed the trencher of meat was half-empty. The breadbox had likewise suffered considerable shrinkage of contents, in company with the sack of dried apples.

"That ties it for shore!" he muttered. "Was she fixin' to come back, she wouldn't pack grub." His visit to the bedroom flashed before his eyes. "Or her old jacket an' shoes," he added morosely. "She purely meant it for sartain."

He placed the food on the table and filled a mug with the hot coffee. The savory odors brought an urgent response from a stomach denied all but a cold snack during the past twenty-four hours. Youthful hunger swept over him to banish all other thoughts, for the time being. He hunched over the table like a famine victim rescued at the last moment.

It was a full twenty minutes later that he crammed down a last mouthful and leaned an elbow on the table. Slowly sipping a final mug of coffee, his glance wandered across the fireplace mantel. Sight of the bone-china dishes brought him up straighter. He moved over for a closer look. Yes, they were just as he had placed them the evening before. Even the porcelain brooch was still upside down in one of the cups. That meant that Tenny had probably left before daylight, without noticing them. Otherwise, she would have at least disturbed something, quite possibly have taken at least the brooch with her.

The tail of one wandering eye unconsciously picked up an unfamiliar outline down at the far end of the mantel. He turned his head to focus on the strange object, then walked over to take it in his hand. His eyes lighted. It was the wood block Joe had been carving on for so long a time. Rance felt the first glow of warmth since awakening. A gift from its creator, patiently carved, and all but forgotten until the last moment before the Indian's hurried departure. The only thing the Calapooya had to leave as a lasting memento of true friendship.

"Shore is a prideful thing!" Rance ran his finger along the delicate tracery of limbs binding together what was plainly meant to represent a slim birch sapling and the sturdy body of a scaly-barked fir. The whole thing displayed the reality of painstaking study and artful craftsmanship. "No wonder he dallied out in the woods half the time!" Rance carried it to the light of the open door. His eyes brightened as he noted how the black walnut stain brought out the fir's true likeness. The birch had been rubbed with something that gave it a pale, chalky sheen. "Plumb lifelike natural," he said, turning it in his fingers at arm's length. "Prob'ly had it cached in his bed, was why he made that last hyper inta the cabin. Reckoned to bring it out so'st I'd not oversight it."

He carried the carving back and placed it carefully on the mantel. His admiration of the work grew as each detail impressed itself more firmly in his mind. Truly, a most prideful memory gift! He guessed he wouldn't be forgetful of the Indian for a right smart while, not with anything as handsome as that to dress up his home.

His home! All the light suddenly vanished from his face, leaving it as grim as a barren hillside. He pulled at his tawny forelock. What kind of a home would this ever be again, without Tenny? The empty room closed in again with all its dreary coldness. Even the fire had died out once more. He went back outside, seeing the warm sunshine without feeling it.

Yes, he just had to find her, wherever she went. Find her and bring her back! He swung his gaze in a wide circle, as if expecting inspiration to wave a signal from some overlooked spot. The landscape stared back stolidly. Nothing moved. His eyes dropped to the ground under the rebuke.

"Best git to scannin' for tracks," he advised himself shortly. "There ain't nothin' here. Should be a mite of sign some'eres of whereat she's headin', though, agin I kin find it."

He started circling the buildings, feeling the relief of some direct action. Wider circles led to where she and Joe had come down the creek, and the Indian's single line of moccasin tracks marking his final departure. No help for his search there! He dropped down on a log and scoured his forelock. Best get this scattering of wits haltered, was he to tree anything before night. He felt his thoughts begin to settle down into some semblance of working order. Now, looking at it practical-like,

Tenny wouldn't be hankering after any more sighting of that country over around where Red Whiskers went. Neither would she be liking to take off up the mountain. That sliced it pretty well down to the open country out toward the settlement.

Rance felt mighty shiftless, thinking on how his snarled wits had already cost him an hour's time. He squinted at the mounting sun. Fresh hope prodded him to his feet. A moment later, he was loping toward the pasture, a bridle slung over one shoulder.

This was, of course, the morning when the gray mare felt the long-dormant fires of youth revive in protest against slavish acceptance of silly human whims. Tail in the air and mane flying, she reverted to the spirit of juvenile delinquency at sight of Rance's approach. He felt like the axle in a pinwheel as she fled in erratic circles each time he moved forward. It was a full half-hour before he finally managed to corner her in an angle of the rail fence. Boiling with frustrated anger, he had no sympathy for a weary old mare suddenly reduced to a symbol of faded years. The fact that the dead alder limb shattered into fragments when he whacked her across the ribs didn't make him feel any better toward her.

Again at the barn, he cinched the saddle in place with spiteful jerks. Tenny might get plumb out of the country while he fooled with the jug-headed old mare, bent on costing him half the forenoon, when time was running out like water going over a dam. He canted another glance at the sun. Well, maybe not a full half the forenoon, but enough to raise a preacher's hackles.

He started to mount, his thoughts reverting to Tenny. What if he did find her, only to meet that same obstinate hostility of last night? Upset and angered into running away under cover of early-morning darkness, she might be stubbornly determined to carry out whatever scheme she had in mind. Maybe talking wouldn't do a mite of good. And he couldn't drag her back by force.

"A right smart persuader, now, might help out, should I have such a thing." He tugged at his forelock. "Something liken to yoke her thinkin' to home things." His mind ranged the cabin fixtures. "Hm-m-m, mayhaps Joe's carving, or the pet piny squirrel, which I likely couldn't ketch nohow."

He scowled at the weathered cabin roof. He half turned back toward the mare. Then, midway of the move, the keepsakes from the burned wagon leaped into his mind without warning. Just the thing! That would move her! He looped the bridle reins over a wagon wheel and sprinted for the cabin.

Heel-thumping the gray mare down the trail a few moments later, he finished pinning the porcelain brooch once more inside his shirt pocket. Having it to bolster his account of the other things waiting on the fireplace mantel should, he reckoned, ease her down enough to pay heed to a scad of things he was fixing to say. Meanwhile, his eyes were busily searching for any sign of her passing along the trail, anything that might assure him a reasonable chance of getting on with his intentions.

It made for slow going. Any footprints that there might have been were indistinguishable among the tracks of the prospectors' three horses coming up the trail the previous morning. It was upward of two miles farther on that a faint moccasin print in the mud of the creek crossing brought his yelp of delight. That surely must mean he was right about her heading for the settlement. And being this far from home, she would undoubtedly stick to the trail the rest of the way. All he had to do was catch up with her. It was a heady thought!

Each thump of his heels on the gray mare's ribs roused a fresh vision of Tenny. It was almost like looking at her through Ma's old kaleidoscope. Tenny running out to get a basket of firing chips; a full-throated voice filling the cabin with melody; Tenny racing down the slope to meet him, like some goldy-bright live thing; the soft curve of her throat shadowing down into the buckskin blouse; an armful of wild-flowers piled high against her breast; the funny little nose wrinkles, when she laughed out loud. Wild hope fought with plodding uncertainty as he scanned the trail ahead. A mute cry for help pushed against his lips.

"Tenny! Tenny! Tenny!" he breathed. "Oh, God, please make 'er wait—an' listen! She's all I got!"

A mile on down the creek, his eyes picked up another foot-print outlined in a damp spot. There was no mistake in this clearly defined print of a right foot; even the odd-shaped patch, just ahead of the heel line, was unforgettably familiar. All he could vision was Tenny plodding down the trail some-where ahead. The gray mare jumped into a run under the stinging slash of rein-ends. It was all he could do to keep from running the animal off its feet as his thoughts leaped ex-pectantly around each concealing bend.

Another hour! Another set of footprints crossing the soft mud of a boggy swale. She was getting careless about leaving tracks, he noted. That meant she was tiring. He doubted that she had slept any during the night, upset as she was. He glanced at the sun, slowly creeping up toward high noon. No wonder she was wearied to faintness, the distance she had come after all that had happened to her yesterday.

He hurried on. The rutted trail wound through a scattered growth of alders. His eyes probed every concealing clump of brush on either side for a possible glimpse of a hiding figure. Neither movement nor sound broke the silence.

It was upon rounding a rock-faced point that he broke abruptly out into the open. A narrow, tree-bordered meadow stretched out before him. And at the farther end was Tenny, her buckskinned figure leaning with drooped head against a trailside stump. His excited yell brought her sharply upright. Her face was a white blur in the distance. One hand lifted as if in protest. From the other dangled the small bundle of jacket, with its burden of biscuits, meat, and the badly cracked shoes. She half-turned, as though about to run, then settled back, head flung high in defiance, like some wild animal brought to bay.

"Tenny! Tenny!" Rance galloped up, almost falling off the mare in his eagerness. "I—I did find you."

"Yes." The flat statement followed a weary shake of her head. "But it was unasked," she added.

"I know. That's why I had to come." He tugged at his forelock, one bare foot rubbing the opposite shin. "You'd no right to take off 'thout speakin'."

"What do you care about my rights? You put me off because you are ashamed to be seen with me in town. You go for days on end without speaking a civil word. You leave me to the mercy of any beastly wood-rat that comes along, while you gad around in the hills for fun." The bitter words dripped from her lips like so much acid.

"But Tenny dear—"

"Don't Tenny dear me! All you want is somebody to stay home, month after month, working her fingers to the bone around the cabin. I might as well be a blanket squaw, for all you care. And even a blanket squaw wouldn't put up with the way you left me to face what was forced onto me yesterday. You men are all alike! You think women are merely creatures of convenience, something not worth a shred of decent consideration. Well, I don't have to put up with it any longer.

I'm going to the settlement. Maybe I can find something out there besides stubborn meanness and beastly sa-savages—" Her voice trailed off in a broken sob.

Rance squirmed like a bee-stung colt. He recognized the truth in her words, even though he reasoned she was laying it on a mite thicker than was needful. Still, there was plenty that edged in uncomfortable close. It would take a heap of easy-talk between them to sort it all out for proper judging. Best let it lay for the time being. His hand found her arm, pulling her down beside him at the foot of the stump.

"Now don't be all-out hostile, Tenny," he begged consolingly, his words coming in a rush. "We've just gotta straight-line a few things, 'thout dredgin' up sore blame in the doin'. Our mistakes were wrongin's that only forgettin' will cure. My mad was partly 'cause I halted at takin' you to town, where gossipy tongues might shame you for stayin' up here alone with me all winter. The other part was all your shyin' off, liken you purely hated me. I went off yesterday to give your folks a buryin'. I aimed to tell you all about it last night, but you was jugged up in the bedroom so'st I couldn't. Nothin' but our own oddments shifted us apart. A mite of common-sense soap'll wash them all out, was we to git our feet on solid ground an' both push in the same d'rection."

"But I am not going back. I should have left ages ago. I knew it all the time, but I was such a coward about parting with the only home and happiness I could ever hope to—"

"Stop it!" He shook her shoulders roughly. "You're no coward! Never was. You saved my scalp an' Joe's life. You stood up as the spunkiest gal't ever lived. Now you gotta come back—back home; there's nothin' there with you gone. It's terrible! Right down dismal as when Pa an' Ma were taken."

Her steady brown eyes lifted hesitantly. She studied his

face for a long moment, while a lone tear inched itself slowly down her cheek. Uncertainty puckered her brow while her fingers twisted themselves together in her lap.

"It grieves me, too, Rance." She spaced her words tremulously. "I'll miss the cabin, with all the nice things we—you have there—and you, your kindness in doing so much for me—and the pine squirrel—and Joe—and—"

"Joe's gone."

"Oh? When was that?"

"Last night. Said his reckonin' was finished. He headed back to his people. But," memory waved its flag for attention, "he left us that thing he's been whittlin' on all this stretch of time. Right handsome it is, too."

"What did it turn out to be?"

"It's—it's a—" A great blinding light suddenly exploded over Rance's head. He gulped. "Why—why, it's you an' me!" he finally got out, his words stumbling over dawning realization of the gift's significance.

He quickly described the unique carving. His interpretation of the work gained strength and breadth of scope as the full extent of its meaning engulfed him. The big, roughly barked fir represented him; Tenny was the slim, leaning birch. The intertwined branches would tie them together for ever and ever.

"Don't you see?" he exclaimed at last. "That lacin' of the limbs together stands for all the aftertimes when naught kin ever sep'rate us. And it's liken to be a right true sign, prob'ly spirit-told right out of his medicine. Everybody claims as how Injuns have a powerful gift for foretellin'." He looked up expectantly.

But Tenny's headshake was obdurate. "It could as easy be wrong," she objected. "Signs and omens are mostly guesswork. Anyway, it wouldn't be right for us to go on living there alone.

Folks would shame us both, once they found out we were not—not nowise related. I couldn't bring you harm like tha—"

"Why, Tenny," Rance broke in, his wide eyes revolving like a pair of sky-blue marbles caught in a whirlwind, "we will be related! That's what I've been tryin' to tell you all this while. Can't you see it? With me lovin' you liken I do, an' allus have, I couldn't leave off marryin' you any longer'n it takes to tree a preacher."

Tenny wiped an unsteady hand across her eyes, neither of them noticing the streak of dirt left across the bridge of her nose. She straightened up slowly, like a manikin coming reluctantly to life. The jacket-wrapped bundle dropped unnoticed to the ground, as the hand that held it lifted itself to the base of her throat.

"You mean—you mean you want me to mar—?"

"Ain't that what I've been tellin' you I was fixin' to do, 'thout no parleyin', soon's we kin git to town? Pa once spoke of a marryin' preacher livin' there. I reckon's how we kin find him. And Mr. Brunner, at the store, will like as not stake me to some shoes an' an outfit for you aginst the furs I aim to bring in, soon's you're minded to make the trip with me."

"Oh, Rance!" It was a sharp cry of happiness, as she swayed weakly against him. "I've loved you for so long. So terribly long! But you never seemed to notice any—"

"Ain't aimin' to miss noticin' nothin' hereon." He hugged her fiercely against his chest. "You're my dearest an' onliest Tenny, long as I got wind enough to make my mouth flap. I've been a-perishin' of love for—"

He stepped back abruptly, slapping at the sharp sting on his chest. He looked down, feeling of his shirt. Then, with a quizzical grin lighting his face, he began unpinning the porcelain brooch from inside the shirt pocket. The helpful persuader had been completely forgotten. Now, gently pressing it into her hand, he guessed it hadn't been nowise necessary, anyhow. It was with something akin to reverence blurring his voice that he gave her a brief account of its finding.

Tenny's cry of recognition at sight of her mother's brooch pinched Rance's lips down in a wordless prayer of thanksgiving. With her arms wrapped possessively around his neck, some moments later, he pulled his eyes back from the crest of the ridge to the south.

"Tenny, my rightful love," he whispered against her lips, "liken I was just a-fixin' to suggest—"

CHAPTER 21

It was the most beautiful morning that Rance thought he had ever seen. The sun smiled its benediction on all creation bounded by the Beaver Creek watershed. Birds warbled paeans of thanksgiving from every trailside bush. Squirrels chattered their delight in tune with the humming of soft breezes in the treetops. Blue grouse drummed amorously on the greening hillsides. Trilliums and pussy ears nodded approbation in the grassy meadow. Mallards and pintails quacked of romance and distant nesting grounds against a background of tinkling music from the creek. A buxom earth stirred gently, her seductive breath rising in undulating waves of springtime perfume. Over all hung the great blue canopy of sky, the darker hem of its skirts outlining snow-crowned peaks and the rising slopes of blue-green timbered slopes, the latter appearing almost purple in the distance.

Rance let his breath escape gently. Everything seemed too perfect to be overset by unseemly voices. His eyes climbed up through the timber to linger on the serrated skyline. The quickening of his pulse was automatic. It was purely queer how the whole country had taken on such a sudden bursting-out scad of beauty just overnight. He had never seen it so sightly, or so wrapped up in friendliness, like a snuggly house filled with happy voices and wonderous cooking smells.

He twisted half around in the saddle to feast his eyes on Tenny. He hadn't sighted her full-faced since that last creek crossing, twenty minutes back. It seemed like he could never get his fill of just looking at her. Pretty as the valley was, she stood out against it like a diamond-stone in a brass ring. And she never looked more sightly than seated behind his saddle, on that red blanket the younger Mr. Brunner had gifted them for a wedding present.

That had sure been purely handsome of Mr. Brunner to right out give them such a fine blanket, after fitting them both up with marrying clothes, on credit against the later delivery of his furs. Too, his giving them leave to spend the night in his warehouse office, fitted out with a sure 'nough bed, was something to brighten a heap of thoughts over a sizable stretch of time. And all the while, he had been uncommon decent about leaving off with snoopy questions, after Rance had told him where he lived and mentioned Tenny as being a newcomer from Tennessee. You didn't find too many folks liken that, willing to settle for what you hankered to tell, and no laying out their long snouts to root deeper into private things. Yes, it was right down princely of him, something to stir a body's liking.

Yes, sir, Mr. Brunner was a long offset to the preacher's woman. Rance reckoned he never would forget how glad he was when the old lady smelt her bread burning. Otherwise, he must needs have been uncommon rude to get out from under all the prying questions her tongue was a-laying to. A thing liken that made a body mindful of Pa's idea that God should have stretched out the punishment of Lot's wife to salt-cure a scad of other wrong-sighted females.

None of that, however, was worth any thought wasting now. His hand closed involuntarily over the soft fingers resting on his saddle cantle. Once a body had everything he wanted, or needed, other folks' doin's didn't figure to carry much heft. He met Tenny's eyes and thought she must be thinking the same way.

"Halfway home a'ready," he said. "Our home, the likeness of which there ain't no other. That is, 'twill be soon's I git you inta it for keeps."

"I'll keep." She poked a finger into his ribs. "Don't ever expect to find me needing to be hauled home on the rump of a horse again."

"You look mighty sweet back there. I dunno but what I'll take up that haulin' home as a reg'lar thing."

"And have me clawing all the hair off your head, as a lawfully wedded wife has every right to do to a brutal husband who is totally without reason or feeling. No sir, Rance Hardig, you can plan to take the wagon next time."

Rance stopped her mouth with a kiss, during which Tenny dragged him headfirst out of the saddle and the gray mare twisted out from under them in an effort to reach a tempting clump of grass.

It was an ignoble landing. Rance plowed his nose into the ground. Tenny fell on top of him, jamming a hard shoulder into his midriff. The bundle of wedding clothes burst open to shower them both with assorted finery, some of which did little to help Rance's appearance. Then, when he raised up, gasping for air, the gray mare swished her tail insolently across his face. A raucous blue jay added the final touch by creaking derisively from a nearby pine tree.

The two victims got untangled enough to sit up, facing each other, their legs spread out flat on the ground. Rance rubbed the dirt out of his eyes, one hand gently caressing the bloody nose. His grin expanded as he surveyed his disheveled bride.

"Well, Missus Hardig," he said, "for an old married woman,

I'd say you look a mite undignified, if not plumb disreputable."

"Thank you, Pappy Hardig! And as you seem to have trouble sitting on a horse, you might give some serious thought to my suggestion for using a wagon in the future."

Rance caught the bubbling laughter behind the shining brown eyes. It was a caution the way her face lit up every time her witty kickbacks left him dangling. He ruefully combed the pine needles out of his forelock with one finger, his eyes thoughtfully studying the bloodstained digit. Like as not, that peeled nose and backfired joke was what he got for misrepresenting things a mite in filling out the preacher's register. He had felt kind of guilty about that, all along. Quick memory flashed the words before his eyes: "Felicity Gatewood, age sixteen, married to Rance Hardig, age nineteen."

Still, it didn't seem as how the Lord should hold it against him over-much, figuring everything. He hunched himself forward, pulling Tenny into the circle of his arms. His lips found the nuzzly little warm spot where a curl nestled against her neck just behind her left ear. No, a body shouldn't rightfully be blamed for trying to head off any stray chance of objections that might bar Tenny from the home and happiness she wanted. No, sir, he'd do it again, and right prideful, too, even though wrongfully swearing three months onto her age and a full two years onto his own did make a bodacious liar out of him.

The watchful blue jay bobbed its head in a jerky nod of approval. Chattering volubly in a lower voice, it flew on up the trail toward the cabin.